SEEDS AND SUNSHINE

A WRECKED NOVEL

JODI PAYNE
BA TORTUGA

To our wives

THE WRECKED UNIVERSE

Read the Wrecked Novels

Wrecked

Flying Blind

Special Delivery

Seeds and Sunshine

1

Jesus, Matty. I can't do this anymore without you. I'm trying, I swear to God, but I'm...lost.

Shiloh Williams stared into the two fingers of whiskey he'd been nursing for an hour. There was just enough for a sip left. Enough for him to swoosh around and pretend that the lights swirling madly were because he was drunk and not because his eyes were filled with unshed tears.

He came in here to this little hole in the wall every night and sat at the back of the bar. He handed Kris a twenty, took his whiskey to the back booth, and stayed until closing time when it would be too late to disturb Skyler with a phone call, too late to do anything but walk down to the weird little apartment he'd rented on the fourth floor of one of the old downtown buildings.

An apartment, baby? Seriously? You're in a shitty efficiency apartment? My gardener? My baby that could spend hours in the yard, in the garden? In the greenhouse I had built for you?

"Shut up, Matty," he whispered. "I'm so fucking tired."

Shiloh had been exhausted for twenty-six months now.

Worn totally to the bone since Percy's Mission had managed to buck Matty off and hook a horn under his vest. Just as Lane Frost had died, Matty had been gone before they got him off the arena dirt.

Matty'd been gone by the time that Shiloh had climbed into the ambulance.

It was like his soul had bled out with Matty's heart, in Dallas.

Eventually he'd had enough of Texas. Maybe that was why, after damn near two years of insisting there was no possible way, he hadn't argued much when Sky invited him up north for his charity event again.

Now he was here, and he had stayed in Sky's guest room for a month before he'd just sold everything barring the things that Matty's folks had wanted to take and rented himself a place up here. He had all the buckles, the pictures, the shirt Matt had worn the day they got married and the one he'd died in. That was enough.

"Hey, man."

Shiloh knew that kid. He came in with his friends a few times a week and played darts or pool or watched the TV. By this point, he knew a lot of faces, mostly because folks would wander by on the way to the head. This kid was the only one that acknowledged him, though, always giving him a wave before disappearing into the men's room.

He tipped his hat, offering the kid something that should look like a smile even if it didn't feel like one. He got a sunny smile in return, so he must have faked it well.

"Whoops. Occupied." The kid backed out of the back area where the bathrooms were, chuckling and leaned against his booth. "That's always so embarrassing, you know? Going for the doorknob and trying to turn it like four times, and by the time you figure out it's locked someone's shouting at you to wait a minute, which you didn't hear over the music, and you're like, sorry man! Ugh."

He arched an eyebrow, but he got that. "Nice thing about this seat. I know when someone comes out."

The kid blinked at Shiloh sort of like he'd grown a second head or something.

"You okay?" If this kid was fixin' to have a stroke, he was leaving without his last sip.

"Oh!" The kid laughed and shook his head. "Yeah, sorry. I was just thinking how brilliant that is."

That wasn't something that he'd ever heard about himself. "Well, thank you kindly, sir. I appreciate that."

Now go on and let me wallow.

A man hurried past them headed back toward the bar. "You're welcome. My turn!" The kid pushed off the booth and moved away.

He caught himself chuckling. Jesus, what a dork, but there was something harmless about him.

Across the bar the guy's friends were playing darts and one of them did something to make everyone cheer. He couldn't see what it was, but when the kid came jogging out of the bathroom, they pounced on him. "Next round is on you, Tate!"

"What? Dude, Dave did *not* win while I was gone. Someone cheated. This is a setup!" The kid—Tate—was laughing, eyes wide, but he was already pulling out his wallet. "I demand a rematch."

"Rematch! Rematch!"

Christ, he remembered being that young and happy. Sort of. A long time ago.

Maybe.

Shiloh sighed softly and finished his drink. Time to go. He had reruns of Iron Chef America to watch.

2

Tate woke up on his couch with the TV still on from the night before. He stretched and sat up, then dug around in the cushions until he found the remote to shut it off. The morning news was both too chipper and too depressing before coffee.

He got up, folded the blanket, and hung it over the back of the couch, fluffed up the cushions and put the remote on the coffee table. He started the coffee maker, set a mug on the counter, and padded to the bathroom in his boxers.

A normal morning, until he looked out the window and saw a handful of cows in his side yard.

He sighed and finished brushing his teeth. That was his own fault. He'd rigged a makeshift fix to that weak section of fence, and he'd planned to mend it right over the weekend.

Silly cows.

He went into the bedroom to get dressed, walking past the neatly made queen-sized bed that he never slept in, and pulled on jeans, a flannel, and his beat-up Timberlands, and then headed outside. It wasn't cold yet, but this morning was chillier than he'd expected.

He rounded the house, looking for Daisy. She was the one everyone would follow. But before he spotted her, he ran into Nash.

"Hey, man. Sorry about this. I got lazy."

His...hand? Milker? Cowboydudefriend?...chuckled. "No worries, boss. I'll get the fence mended later. Daisy! Get your butt back to the damn barn!"

"Yeah? I would appreciate that. I'm driving for the brewery tonight after school." It took a lot of jobs to float this place, but he didn't mind. He loved it. But sometimes after teaching teenagers all day long he could be pretty wiped.

"Busy-busy. You have anything you need me to do, specifically?" Nash got the last of the cows out of the front yard.

"Just the usual today. Feed and all, maybe have a look around with winter in mind? Do we have kittens yet?" Fred, his big orange barn cat, was apparently not a boy. He'd had to assume a gender because Fred was a good mouser, but not so into people.

"I bet so. She's gone poof, and her food is disappearing. I keep hunting them."

"Well, at least it's not too cold. We can offer her a blanket if you find them. Are you hungry? I was about to make some eggs before I take off." He needed to eat before teaching the kids. It took a lot of energy to get teenagers excited about geometry first period.

"Sure, if you're cooking. You know my guy's position on the kitchen." Yeah, Nash's boy toy was...more decorative than functional.

"Your positions in the kitchen are definitely no business of mine. Come on." They closed the cows in and headed back to the house. "Coffee's hot." He poured them each a mug as soon as they got inside. "He's still your guy, huh?"

"So far." Nash glanced at him, and they shared a wicked grin. "I got to admit, he's got an awful pretty mouth..."

He snorted, cracking eggs. "You're something else. Can he drink legally yet?"

"Shut up."

"That's a no."

"Only for three more months."

Nash was good-looking and had a great smile. Tate was tempted once, for about five minutes. As tempted as he ever was by anyone. But Nash was a bit of a horndog, and he didn't need that in his life. At least he didn't think so. Well, he totally didn't want it.

And with his thirty-first birthday a few weeks away, he was pretty sure he was meant to be an old, salty, Vermonter one day. Someone the kids would call "Old Man Dutton." He kind of liked it. He had friends, he had a social life, he wasn't hiding his head in the sand. He just...wasn't the romantic type. Or something.

He split the scrambled eggs in half and put them on plates just as the English muffins popped up. He put one on each plate and set them on the table. "There's butter...oh and we need forks."

"Got it!" Nash grabbed two out of the dish drainer, doing this weird-assed little dance that had him laughing hard, leaning on the table to balance himself.

"You're a nut, man." He took a fork from Nash and sat down. "I was going to invite you to the bar tonight, but you can't bring your pretty young thing with you."

"He's got class."

"His GED?" He couldn't help himself. He just couldn't.

"Shut up, boss!"

"Uh-huh. How many guys can say that and not get fired, huh?" He was grinning; he loved teasing Nash.

"This one. You adore me. You know it. No one loves your cows more than I do."

"Let's not get kinky, now. I don't want to hear from Daisy that you're putting the moves on her."

"Dude! Dude, I only like boys. No. Udders."

He cracked up. "Jesus, I need more coffee to keep up with you." He shoveled in a big bite of eggs and chewed happily. He had it good. "Well if he needs a math tutor, I'm your guy."

"No way, man. You're a hot teacher. He's probably got a fantasy about that..."

"Doesn't everyone? Oh, except you. You're busy seducing students." He popped the last bite of his English muffin into his mouth and scooped up their plates. It was about time to go.

"Nah. He was legal and a dropout." Nash waggled his eyebrows. "Have a good day, teach."

"You too, Nash. Help yourself if you need lunch." Tate didn't lock the back door; no one around here did, and after a couple of years of working together, he trusted Nash anyway. He grabbed his keys and his backpack and headed out into the sunshine.

3

"Hey, Whiskey." The bartender winked at him, pushing over his glass.

"Sir. How goes it?"

Shiloh didn't really listen to the answer, but he did tip his hat and nod. He wasn't sure about being somewhere long enough to have a nickname.

It just felt weird.

Not as weird as someone being in his goddamn booth, though. He knew it was unreasonable to be pissed off, but he was.

That was his spot.

Every night.

Not a bunch of goofy-assed boys.

Shiloh sighed dramatically and went to sit at the end of the bar so he could wait them out. He was being ridiculous. He knew this, but he couldn't help it.

That was his booth, where he sat and talked to Matty.

"...but it's been a good day. You want some pretzels?" The bartender, whose name he probably should have asked weeks ago but didn't, grabbed a basket of those little sticks and sat it in front of him.

"Thanks."

You know, this is all your fault, Matty. If you hadn't died, I'd be sitting on our front porch with a glass of tea. I didn't even know I liked whiskey, really.

"We need another round, please, Tom." Four empty pint glasses landed on the bar.

"Four Heady Toppers? Thanks for these." The bartender —Tom—picked up the empties and put them in the dishwasher, then pulled out four new glasses.

"Nothing but the best!"

"No pool tonight?"

"It's been a long week; we decided to sit this one out." Deep blue eyes turned on him and he got a smile. "Hi."

"Evenin'." He nodded, lips quirky. If he had his booth, he wouldn't have folks talking to him.

"I've seen you in here a bunch of times. I'm Tate." Great. Now the guy wanted to shake hands.

"Shi—"

"That's Whiskey right there," the bartender interrupted, and he had to fight himself not to explode.

"I'm just waiting for my normal booth to open."

"Oh—"

Tom chuckled and pointed to Tate. "He's in it."

Tate blinked, looking confused. "Oh...uh. Right, that's why I recognize you. We're uh...you want to join us?"

"No. No, y'all look like you're having fun." And he was not. He wasn't in a having fun space. He was needing an hour outside his apartment to talk to Matty and watch life go on and on.

"We are. We're just goofing around. You seem like you might need a little fun. Or company? Something." Tate was sincere, he could tell, and maybe he did need company, but he didn't want it.

"Thanks, man, but I'm just going to keep myself and my mood away from others. Thank you for the offer, though."

"Take it from me, man. You're going to be okay. I know, I'm like, nobody, but I know."

"Four IPAs." Tom set the glasses on the bar, and Tate picked up three. "I'll be back for that one."

Tate carried the three beers, carefully balancing the third glass, all the way to the back booth.

His booth.

Dammit.

See? This is what I get for mentioning to the little twink last time about how my seat was the best, Matty. If I'd just kept my mouth shut, I wouldn't be stressing it right now.

There was a round of laughter coming from his corner, and then Tate was back. The kid picked up the beer and took a long sip...

Then sat down on the barstool right next to him.

Okay... Okay, what was this?

Did people do that?

Sit close?

"So...what's your sport? Ice hockey? Skiing? Basketball?"

The question made him look around to see who the kid was talking to, and then he figured out it was him. "Rodeo, mostly. I mean, I know football and baseball..."

"Rodeo. That's unusual for up here." Tate took another sip of his beer and shifted on his stool like he was trying to get a better look. "Where are you from?"

"Outside Austin." He wasn't from here. He liked it, though. It was different and quiet and smaller in so many ways. Or maybe it was him that was smaller...

"That's a long way." Tate just nodded, and he didn't ask

what Shiloh had expected next. The same question everyone asked. Tate didn't ask why. "Is Austin cool? I've never been."

"It is, in some ways. Not the weather. At all." In fact, the weather could be intense—hot and humid and melty.

"The weather here can be intense too."

He didn't doubt it. Sky said the winters were wild. "Yeah. Lots of snow and all."

"I guess you don't get much snow down in Austin." Tate chuckled and tapped his beer glass, looking a little awkward as he tried to make conversation. "Makes driving fun."

Goddammit. Sometimes it was hard, being polite. "It might snow for a few seconds every five or six years, but mostly, if there's a winter storm, it's ice... Y'all get ice storms?"

"Some. Mostly it's cold enough to be snow here. A lot of snow." Tate glanced at him again. "Do you...want to shoot some pool?"

"Thanks, kid, but I'm not good at shit like that." Whether or not that was true, he wasn't good at having fun. Not anymore.

Tate's blue eyes flashed at him. "Which, pool or flirting?"

"Shit." It came out shee-it, just as long and drawling as hell. "I haven't flirted in so long I don't even remember how."

"Well," Tate drawled back playfully, smiling at him. "I'll give you a tip. I'm flirting. Now. With you. You could just... follow my lead."

"I'm an old man. You got a table full of pretty over there."

"They're handsome. And they're just friends. But it's good to know I've read you right."

"Yeah, I'm about as queer as a three-dollar bill."

Tate snorted. "You really should sound much more proud of that fact."

He didn't follow. "What?"

"Sorry. I don't know, I thought I heard you sigh. You're not old, you know."

"I feel ancient." *Shut up, man!*

"See? That's what I mean. I don't know anything about Austin, but Vermont is welcoming. This bar is welcoming. You should look around you, you know?"

Look around? Him? His heart was broken, and he wasn't sure it would ever be okay. Ever. "I—I'm not ready. I'm sorry. I lost—I'm not—" He stood up, his throat working. "I got to go. Sorry, man. See you later."

Then he ran. It was his only choice.

He had to go home before one drink became a bottle became a bullet.

He didn't have another option.

4

Tate pulled into the parking lot and parked his truck. It had been a long week at school, and he was ready for a distraction and maybe some pool. Clinton's was busy, and the music hit him as soon as he pulled the door open, making him smile.

"Tate's here!" Kent gave him a wave from the pool table where he was probably cleaning up.

"Gonna get a beer," he mouthed, figuring Kent wouldn't be able to hear him. Nobody could shout like Kent.

He weaved around tables on his way to the bar to order a beer, letting himself glance over at that corner booth to see if the handsome Texan was in it.

Cowboy hat pulled down, black button up open at the neck, glass of whiskey in front of him. Oh yeah. He was right there.

And the man was just as sexy as the other day, even without being able to see the guy's face.

"IPA?"

"Yes, please." He nodded to Tim. "Cowboy got his booth back, huh?"

"He did. That is an unhappy dude, man. But he tips every single night, never gets drunk, and he never makes trouble."

"Yeah." After the way the guy had torn out of the bar the other day, unhappy didn't seem like a strong enough word. Tate watched the way he tapped the side of the whiskey glass with one finger but didn't pick it up, wondering how long it would take him to drink it. "He only ever drinks one?"

"He doesn't even drink it half the time. He just buys it and sits." Tim shrugged and offered him a half sigh. "He really seems like a decent guy."

"He does, right? I thought maybe I could get him talking but..." He shrugged. "I probably should leave him alone, huh?" Should...but...

"He's not my type, so go for it." Tim chuckled. "He eats the pretzels."

"Ha." No, he was Tim's type, but he wasn't into Tim. "Pretzels, huh? Maybe. Has he said anything to you? Like... why he's all the way up here from Austin? What he does for a living, or anything?"

"Nope. He never says anything personal. He sits there for an hour, maybe two, with that one glass. He'll eat the pretzels. I mean, I run his credit card, so I know his name, but I call him Whiskey. He's got to be friends with that cowboy dude that has the rodeo bull thing, right?"

"Oh yeah?" He glanced over again. Something about the cowboy just pulled him right in. He could just stare for ages. "Yeah, maybe so." He took a big sip of his beer and slid off his stool, then scooped up a bowl of pretzels.

Food was a good icebreaker, right?

The guy was pale as a sheet as he came up, and he almost didn't stop, but everyone needed a friend, right?

He set the pretzels down carefully and slid them into the cowboy's line of vision. "Hey."

"Shit!" The man jerked, almost knocking over his glass, catching it with his fingertips. "Whoa. Sorry. I was woolgathering."

"Is that like, spacing out?" He was glad he hadn't set his beer down yet.

"Just like, yes." He got a quick glance. "Thanks for the pretzels."

His heart pounded briefly at the sight of those dark eyes. "You looked hungry." What? Why did he say *that*? "I mean... uh." He sat without asking permission and instantly felt awkward about it. "Something wrong with your drink?"

"No. No, I just like to stretch it out. It's a waste of whiskey and money to just shoot it back."

"I guess that depends on why you're drinking." He grinned and touched his glass to the whiskey glass before taking a sip.

"You have a point." Was that a half-smile? Maybe?

"So...we got interrupted last time. I'm Tate, and you're...?" He returned the smile, hoping to keep the lighter vibe going.

"Shi."

Well, he knew that. The guy was a fortress.

"You think? I'd say more reticent than shy..."

"Huh?" He got the most curious look.

What? Had he missed something? He hadn't had that much beer. "You...said you were shy?"

"Yeah." The man frowned, then rubbed the bridge of his nose. "No. I mean, I am. Named, that is."

"Named...oh! Oh my god. I'm so sorry." He shook his head, trying not to laugh, but it was a losing battle, and the giggles broke through. "Jesus. I'm an idiot."

Shy—really, that was a name?—winked at him over the table. "Well, we were both confused as all get out."

That wink was so warm and so sexy he stopped giggling. "This is my first beer, I swear." He could sit here for a while, maybe have another, see if he could keep Shy talking.

"This is my first too." Shy lifted his still-full glass, swirling the whiskey in the tumbler.

First and only. That's what Tim had said. "Don't you get bored, sitting here all night?"

"Not really. This is my social hour."

Was that sarcasm?

He snorted. He didn't think sitting alone in a busy bar counted as social, but to each his own. "Is this what passes for social in Texas?"

"It can, yessir. I'm out and about, I'm dressed, and I'm talking to you. See? Social."

That was unexpectedly adorable. He nodded. "Okay, then." If they were talking, then he was going to ask what he really wanted to know. "So why Vermont?"

"Guess."

Oh, okay. Okay, that was unexpected.

"What? Really?" He chuckled, grinning. "Uh...you love snow." Ridiculous. Nobody from Austin was going to love snow.

Shy trailed his finger around the rim of the glass. "I haven't seen much of it yet, but I hope I do. Otherwise I'll be moving. I came out because a friend lived here."

"Oh! The rodeo guy, I bet. Right? Tim thought so." Tim read people so well. It was probably a bartender thing. "Do you ride? Rope? Something?"

The color drained out of Shy's face again. "No. No, I am... I don't. I was a fan."

Was? Shit, he'd walked right into something. "I've been a

couple of times to watch. It's a lot of fun." Damn it. Whatever he'd said had sent those warm, dark eyes back into the glass of whiskey.

"To that event? It takes a lot to put it on."

"Yeah. I mean, it's local, you know? It's one of the few big things drawing people up here during mud season. I thought it was great. I'm right then? You're friends with uh... Paulson isn't it? The guy who runs it."

"Yeah. He's a good man. We're like family." *Like* family, but not family.

"Cool. So you're here...maybe to help with the event?" *Can you look at me again?* He really thought they were starting to hit it off.

"It's in May, but I might. I don't know."

"Well, you've got time to figure it out." Tate let silence fall for a minute, and Shy didn't seem to mind it. He seemed very occupied with his whiskey. "Hey, if I said something I shouldn't have... I'm sorry."

"No. No, it's an anniversary of... It's just a hard day for me. It was brave, to try and cheer me up, kiddo."

Do you think you're scary? "I'm sorry it's a tough day. But I wasn't being brave; I was just flirting with a hot cowboy." He smiled, even though Shy wasn't looking at him. "And I like you."

Shy glanced up, and those cheeks went pink. "You are something else, but thank you. That's good to know. When I remember how to flirt, you'll be the first to know."

"That sounds fair." That also sounded like a very polite request to be left alone, and he didn't want to push too hard on a bad day. He slid out of the booth, taking his empty beer glass with him. "Good talking to you again. I bet I know where to find you next time."

"Yeah, I bet you do. I'll be right here."

Something about that statement made him sad for the cowboy. "If you decide you want company or an ego boost, I'll be over there. I'm really bad at pool."

"Have a great night, kiddo. Thanks for the company." He got an actual, literal tip of the hat.

He nodded back but sighed as he turned away. *Kiddo.* Not exactly the impression he'd been trying to make.

"What's with you and the cowboy? Are you finally going to play?"

He glanced up at Kent and found a smile. "You just like taking my money."

"How do you think I pay for my beer?"

He snorted and picked up a cue, shaking Shy off for the night. "Let's do it, then."

5

_____

"Shiloh Williams, I swear to god, if you keep avoiding me and the kids, I'm going to tell Charlie you're an axe murderer."

Shiloh stared at Skyler Paulson, shocked and not that the bull rider would be sitting across from him at the table, all at the same time. "Are you stalking me?"

"Yep!" Skyler sat down with a pair of beers. "Beck is parking the truck. We're child-free for the weekend."

"And you're hanging here with me? Are you stupid?" That was sweet and a little misguided, but the guys had three kids. They needed adult time.

"It's early yet. And we get to hang out with adult friends. Don't worry, we have a hotel room up the block. Walking distance. We're not that stupid." Sky sipped his beer.

"Good men. You should enjoy it." He swirled his whiskey and found Sky a smile. "How are y'all doing?"

"Charlie misses you."

He took a taste of his whiskey. That was a pretty heavy guilt trip. "Pulling out the big guns?"

"I am. You've turned down dinner invitations, concert

tickets, movie nights...you've left me with no choice. I'm running out of things to tell her to cover for you. Yesterday I told her you might have been eaten by lions."

"Oh. Well, somehow I think she would come and rescue me. Can I come to supper next week? I'll bring pizza." He could handle a lot, but not hurting a kid, especially not one that seemed to honestly love him.

"Yes. Come Tuesday early, like five. Beckett works from home on Tuesdays."

"We have Tuesday plans?" Beckett was tall and handsome, and Shiloh noticed the clean shave, the man was ready for date night.

"Shiloh is bringing pizza. Hey, you." Skyler gave Beckett a quick kiss. "Got you a beer."

"Thank you." Beckett looked at him seriously. "Now, remember what I told you. Smitty's has the best pizza and be sure to order zeppoles. Charlie frowns when I forget."

If it really made Charlie frown, he doubted Beckett forgot much.

"I won't forget. I swear, guys. I've just been settling in." He hadn't been good company.

He hadn't been company at all.

"You've been brooding. It ain't good for you, man." Sky had that hangdog serious look down. "It ain't right."

"Bah. I'm just a little off." And he thought maybe he always would be.

"Hey, man. Check it out, you have company!" Tate—he was surprised to find he remembered the kid's name—gave him the usual smile but stopped at the edge of the booth. "I always see him by himself. I'm glad to see he's found some company."

Glad? Why would the kid even care?

"Yeah? Shiloh here is alone too much. He needs

company. He's new to town, you know?" Sky warmed to his story, even as Shiloh kicked him under the table. "He came to visit us, and he stayed. Got him a little apartment close by."

"I knew he had to be near the bar; I see him every time I'm in here. Usually getting my butt kicked at pool." Tate laughed easily, turning warm eyes on him. "Shiloh, huh? That's what Shy is short for?" Tate offered a hand.

"Mhm." He shook it. He was going to murder Sky in his sleep.

He might even enjoy it.

Tate blinked at him. "Wow, those are some hands." Tate let go slowly. "Strong."

"Thank you." Was he? He supposed so, or he had been, once upon a time.

"You're welcome." Tate tapped the table. "I was on my way to the little boys room, so...nice meeting you all. Come over and play some darts later if you want. Or pool."

"Pool?" Beckett's eyes lit up. "Maybe I'll come over in a bit."

"The more the merrier. I better scoot before it's an emergency!" Tate waved and took off.

"Oh, do you play darts, Shi?" Sky asked.

"No." He wasn't sure he ought to be given sharp pointed objects.

"I bet he'd teach you; I mean if you're both here that often, you know?" Beckett was getting in on the game now.

"Shut up. He's what? Six and a half? Seven? I've got chaps older than him!"

"He's got be at least twenty-one, right? And I wasn't setting you up; I was suggesting you do something other than sit here all night."

Well, that was direct.

"Y'all... You don't understand. I don't know what to do without him. What do to with my time." He was so goddamn bored.

"Get a job?" Beck replied quickly. "Volunteer?"

"Doing what, man?" He was qualified to do what? Dig in the dirt? He didn't know how to grow things in the snow.

"Not feeling sorry for yourself."

"I didn't expect to be ambushed when I came here tonight."

"I'm just trying to—"

Beckett touched Sky's arm, and Sky gave his husband a raised eyebrow but stopped talking. Beck went on instead. "Shiloh, listen. You came from a ranch. This is cow country. Horse country. In the snow, okay, but how different can it be?"

"I don't know, man, but I'll think about it, okay? Seriously?" He would, but he didn't have to like it.

Beckett nodded. "Cool. Good."

Tate walked by again, not stopping, just giving him a smile this time as he headed back to the bar. The kid ordered his usual IPA on tap—and rejoined his crew.

Why did he even know the kid's usual?

"We should go play darts."

"I suck at darts, Sky, but the three of us can play pool..." Beck offered.

Yeah, he wasn't getting suckered into that. "I'm good. You two go ahead."

Beckett and Skyler exchanged a look, and he braced himself.

Sky sighed, staring at him with a hound dog expression. "I'm worried about you, buddy."

"I—" He was too, but it was like he was stuck now.

"I'm going to see about some pool." Beckett stood up suddenly, squeezed Sky's shoulder and left.

"Guess he thinks we'll talk better without him." Sky shrugged at him. "So?"

"I'll look for a job, okay? I'll do that."

"Look. I get it, Shi, you know I do. A job is a good start, it's a reason to get out of bed, right? It's been two years; Matthew would want you to move on. Hell, he'd be kicking your ass right now if he could and you know it."

"I just...he was everything." He held Skyler's gaze. "I stopped being just me. I was an *us*, man. I don't know how to go back."

"You can't. You can't go back; you can only go forward, and figure out who you are now. But sitting here in a bar half the day and sleeping off the other half isn't who you are. You know that."

"I miss him." And that was the truth.

"I miss you." Sky winked at him, but his smile was gentle. "If you need help, man. Get it. Don't just fade into nothing. My kids like you."

He chuckled, but his face was on fire. "For chrissake, let's go play some goddamn pool, Sky."

"Now you're talking." Sky slid out of the booth. "Let's go kick that kid's ass."

Beckett was on deck for a game that looked like it was just about ending. "Oh, look who decided to play." Beckett winked at him and handed him the cue he'd been holding. "You take my place, Shiloh. I'm going to dance my husband around a little."

"I can do that. Y'all have fun." He shook his head, but he took the cue. At least he did remember how to shoot pool.

"Hey! You have a cue. Are you up?" Tate's voice came from behind him, and then Tate himself appeared at his side. In this light he could really see the kid's deep blue eyes. "Oh, you're going to play Kent. He's good."

"Would you like to take my place?" It seemed the nicest thing to offer. Not that he was worried about losing. He could shoot a game of pool. Absolutely.

"Absolutely not. I told you I'm no good at pool. I'll watch." Tate leaned against the pool table, smiling. "Maybe you can teach me something."

"It's unlikely." He offered this Kent a mild smile, a nod. "You want to break, or should I?"

"Newcomer breaks, man." Kent looked about the same age as Tate, but he was tall and thin, and his hair was dark and much longer.

"Fair enough." He lined up and broke, sinking two stripes and a solid. "Looks like I'm stripes."

Tate clapped his hands. "Whoa, nice."

"Looks like it." Kent nodded and scanned the table, nodding slowly. "Nice break."

"Yes, sir." It didn't take long before he sank three more and scratched.

"Ooh. Tough break." Kent pulled out the cue ball and set it on the table, setting himself up to sink one solid and then one more after that. The next shot was tricky, and Kent circled the table, looking for the best move.

"Where did you learn to play pool?" Tate stepped up beside him again. "I learned right here in this bar."

"I spent a lot of time on the road in bars." A lot. And he'd dealt with a shitton of pool sharks.

Kent found a shot, lined it up and took it, sinking another solid.

"On the road?" Tate's head tilted. "Were you with a band?"

"Who me? No. No, my husband was a bull rider." A band. Him. God. Skyler would die laughing.

"No way, really? That's what you were talking about the other night."

"Yeah." And dangerous, but that wasn't a surprise. Men got hurt. It happened. Men died for the rush.

"So you're from Austin...where is your husband from?"

"Matt was from Louisiana. He wouldn't have liked it up here. He was a bayou baby." And a happier man you'd never meet.

"Wouldn't have...oh. Damn. When you said... I mean I figured he was retired or something but... I'm so sorry."

Kent sank another solid, but he missed the next one, it stopped just shy of dropping into the far corner pocket. "Ah, damn it. All yours."

"You're good, man." But he was better. He finished the game off—boom, boom, boom. "And no worries, Tate. You didn't know. It's all good."

Tate and Kent both stood there blinking at him.

"I better shake your hand. Not too many people beat me around here." Kent stuck a hand out. The words weren't bragging, just like he was stating a fact. Kent didn't really have a competitive vibe.

"Of course, man." He shook Kent's hand, gave the man a smile. "You want to play again, you just holler."

"He beat Kent?" A young man in a UVM T-shirt gaped at Tate.

Tate nodded, grinning. "Yeah, he did."

"Kent, you're finally buying drinks!" Tate's group of friends were suddenly around Shiloh, giving him pats on the back and shaking his hand. "Way to go, man."

Tate waved to the group. "This is Shiloh, everybody. Isn't that a great name?"

"You're famous now, Shiloh. At least in this little bar."

He chuckled, and it felt so odd, to mean it, to feel something easy. "Thanks, y'all. I appreciate it."

A server brought over a tray of beers and one whiskey, and Kent lifted the whiskey off the tray and handed it to him. "Whiskey. For the pool shark. Not a beer man, huh?"

Kent held out a beer to Tate, but Tate refused. "Thanks. School night."

"Are you a student?" That wouldn't surprise him a bit. Tate was adorable, fresh-faced and cute.

Tate laughed. "I know, I look young, huh? I'm a teacher. I teach high school math. I'm older than I look, I swear."

"Oh? Oh, no shit? Wow. Lucky man. You look like a kid." He knew he sounded shocked, but dammit, he was.

"I know." Tate blushed a little, shaking his head. "Even my students say that. You should see the looks on their parents' faces on conference night."

"I bet. I'd have said you were just barely drinking age." His genetics weren't that glorious, and he'd been letting his heart drag on his face, he knew.

"I figure when I'm sixty I'll appreciate it, but right now, it's kind of a drawback." Tate glanced around. "Are you playing another round? You want to go sit? I've got a few minutes before I need to head home."

"I'm done, but sure." He glanced around, but Sky and Beck had disappeared, either in the shadows or out to the hotel, he didn't know.

He wasn't sure he cared.

Tate led him back to his usual booth. "It was good to meet your friends. It has to be good to be around them, right? And kids...it's hard not to be present with kids around. Good for you."

"Yes. They have a six-year-old, a four-year-old, and one

that's just gone two years old." And every so often Sky teased Beckett about having 'just one more.'

"Wow. That's a handful. Was that Sky you were with earlier?"

"Yes, sir. He was the little guy. Beck's the tall dude, his husband." He was comfortably normal—not tall, not short, not heavy, not skinny. Brown hair, brown eyes, a couple of tattoos—just a normal dude.

"Do they ride? You don't..."

"I can ride a horse, for sure. I grew up on a cotton farm, though. Cotton and soybeans. Sky used to ride, but he was in a bad wreck—sort of like my husband, except Sky made it. Beck's a lawyer."

"Wow. That's a lot of real world." Tate chuckled, then sipped his beer looking thoughtful. "I guess I'm just used to my rural high school and my little farm."

"Hey, before I met Matt, I had been just as far as Dallas. I get it." He'd been given a crash course in traveling and hotels and rodeo cowboys and wild sex. It had been terrifying and the most fun he'd ever had.

"Oh, I bet that had to be crazy. They go all over those cowboys. Seems like they're somewhere new every weekend. It looks exhausting." Tate was so genuine; he really seemed interested, not like it was just small talk.

"It's a different life, for sure. Eventually we bought a ranch—somewhere I could work, but it's gone now."

"I bet you miss it." Tate shifted just so, and the light caught his eyes in a flash of blue. "Was that your work? What did you do on your ranch? I have cows. A little land."

"I'm a gardener by trade, but we ran horses and cattle, some chickens and goats. I mainly grow things, though."

"But you live local now right? You don't have a farm anymore?"

"I'm on the fourth floor of the old bank building. Just a little place." It wasn't forever, but it was a place for his suitcase.

"You know, maybe this is forward but... I have a bunch of land. Like it's sitting fallow. I'd be happy to let you use some of it." Tate shrugged. "I don't want to make you uncomfortable but if you're interested, it's just me out there...and some cows."

"What do you want done with it?" Why would anyone just offer to let him borrow some land? How much land? Was it good land?

"I don't know. You're the gardener." Tate grinned. "I just live there. And my buddy Nash helps out with the cows and does...handy stuff. I work a second job sometimes, so he's... well, handy." Tate chuckled and shook his head. "I think I must be getting tired."

"Well, I can come and look at the property, make a couple three suggestions for you? Maybe draw you up a planting plan..." He was interested to see another piece of property.

"Hand me your phone?"

"Okay..." He handed his phone over with a grin. "Make sure you put your name on your contact."

"That would be just like me, to not to remember to put my name in." Tate tapped on his phone, entering his information, then handed it back. The contact read "Tate Dutton" and there was a phone number and an address. "Normally I don't just hand out my address but I'm pretty sure that Sky friend of yours you were talking about earlier is the same retired bull rider that runs the event in May, which makes you both incredibly cool, and probably trustworthy."

"It is the same retired bull rider, yes. I came up originally to a memorial for the fallen bull riders."

"Oh wow. Like for your husband? That had to be something." Tate slid out of the booth. "I want to hear about it, but I have to be up for school early, so I'm going to head out. If you decide you want to have a look, give me a call, or stop by if you want to. Nash will probably be there if I'm not."

"I'll call. Thanks, man." He needed to get out of here too. It was time to head home, play a few hours on his phone and crash.

"Good to finally meet you for real. Don't hide back here anymore. We don't bite." Tate grinned and headed off, saying goodbye to his buddies as he made his way to the door.

No, they didn't bite, and it was good to talk to people who didn't know him, didn't know Matty. It was...different, but good.

He thought about that, all the way back to the apartment.

6

———————

T ate hadn't made it to the bar last night. After school he did some deliveries for the local brewery, his second job, and by eight o'clock he was toast. He usually was on Fridays, keeping up his energy for those kids all week could wear him out.

But it was Saturday morning, and all he had to do today was grade his end-of-week quizzes. He planned to get out and chop some wood at some point too—winter was coming and there was work to do to get ready for the cold and the snow.

But right now he was keeping warm in his barn coat while sipping his coffee on the porch and scrolling through social media on his phone like he had nothing better to do. The sun was out, but it was that time of year when mornings and evenings were chilly, even if the day warmed up nicely.

His phone buzzed, surprising him, and it was Shiloh, the pretty, sad cowboy with the gorgeous dark eyes.

> Hey, man, if you want me to stop by this weekend, holler.

Well, that was cool. He hadn't been convinced Shiloh would get in touch. Still, it sounded like the cowboy thought he was asking for a favor, when really he was trying to do one for Shiloh.

> I'm around today, just grading and doing some cleanup around the place.

> I'm free. You like donuts?

He snorted.

> There are people who don't like donuts?

> Not smart people. See you in 1/2 hr?

> Looking forward to it.

He was, actually. For all that Shiloh kept to himself, there was something about him. Something more than hurt in those dark eyes. And he was handsome. Not that there was anything about Shiloh that suggested he was interested in anything other than gardening, and he still wasn't sure the cowboy even wanted to do that.

Doughnuts called for coffee so he put another pot on, then pulled on some jeans and his Timberlands. He was Saturday scruffy, but he didn't think Shiloh would mind.

When a fancy dark pickup pulled up, a rush of excitement hit him. He loved this—something new, someone new and interesting.

Shiloh stepped out of the truck with a box of pastries, wearing a pair of dark jeans and a heavy navy button-down, a black cowboy hat. Such a cowboy.

He stepped off his porch to meet Shiloh partway. "Hey, there." *You look amazing.* "That's a nice truck."

"Thanks. It's new. Great ride and heated seats."

"You'll love those in a couple of months. Welcome to my little place." It wasn't that little actually; he had sixty acres, most mowed and fenced for grazing for the cows but some was left wild. The house was a small farmhouse, well built and cozy but definitely not big.

"It's a pretty piece of land. Seriously." Shiloh seemed more relaxed in the sunshine, outside. The neon lights didn't suit him.

"Thank you. I bought the land and the house not long after college. As soon as I got the job teaching here." He'd kind of fallen in love with the wrap-around porch. "I fixed it up a little, but it wasn't too bad."

"Are you from around here, then?" Shiloh handed him the box.

"Yeah. I grew up in the next town over. It was a good place to grow up, a really liberal, open-minded place, you know?" He took the box and led Shiloh inside. "I made coffee."

"I am a fan of coffee, I admit. Really liberal doesn't sound like bad at all."

"No, it was good. I just couldn't stay there after..." *After the fire.* It had been long enough; you'd think he could just say it now, but he still hesitated every time. "I was at college, and I lost my parents in a fire. It took the whole house."

"Damn, I'm sorry. That sucks." Shiloh offered over a nod, eyebrows crinkling in the middle.

"Thank you." That was somehow just as hard. "Anyway, I had some money, so I bought this place. It's been good. Have a seat." He gestured to the kitchen table. "Tell me about your gardening."

"I've got a degree in landscaping. I tended to create victory gardens, rose gardens, those types of things."

"Well, it's fall and it's going to be cold soon, but if you want to build a greenhouse and see what you can do with it, I've got plenty of room. Be my guest."

"Maybe. Maybe I could..." Shiloh's blush was just enough to make his cheeks rosy.

He smiled and set a mug of coffee down for Shiloh. "You could." He sat across the table and admired the color, and how it made Shiloh's dark eyes shine. "I can ask Nash to help you if you want."

"No. No, if I build something, I won't take your man to do it. That's unkind."

He shook his head and opened the pastry box. "You are very good at saying no, Shiloh."

"I don't know that anyone's ever said that to me before." Shiloh sounded like he wasn't sure if he was amused or not.

"Well...you didn't want to play pool, and then you kicked ass, you didn't want to come out here but you did anyway, and now I'm offering you some help and you won't take it." He grinned, hoping Shiloh would understand his words to be—mostly—in fun.

"It's been a while." Shiloh offered him a tentative smile. "I got a variety. I didn't know which you'd like."

Smiling was good. He'd watched this cowboy frown in the back corner booth at the bar for a while now. This was much better. "There is no bad doughnut." That was the truth. He lifted a jelly one out of the box. "Especially not from this place. Have you tried their raisin bread? It's luscious."

"I have it for breakfast every damn morning."

"Now you're talking. With a little honey? Mm. So good." He sipped his coffee, watching Shiloh relax right before his eyes. "Do you work?"

"I don't, no, and I miss it." Shiloh frowned for a second,

then his face relaxed. "I really do, you know? I miss working. I just... I've been living on his insurance and the whole sales of the ranch money thing."

Jesus. It sounded like Shiloh was stuck in a really lonely limbo. Like...really stuck. "Oh, man. So you...hang out at the bar at night and...what do you do all day?"

"I drink a lot of coffee and watch the Food Network, and god, doesn't that sound like a boring damn life?" This time, the smile climbed right up into Shiloh's dark eyes.

"Well? Yeah. That sounds pretty damn boring." He laughed gently and sipped his coffee. "I know we can do better than that."

"We'll see about that, won't we?" Shiloh took a blueberry doughnut, humming as he took a huge bite.

"Ooh, a challenge. Well, I can show you around the property if you like, scout out a spot for your greenhouse. Nash is off today, so you never know what daily disaster we could run across." The cows were out grazing, and Nash had fixed his lousy quick and dirty fence repair job for him so it hopefully wouldn't be them.

"You said you have a dairy? I've never known any milk cows. We raised beef cattle on the ranch."

Okay, that was surprising. He assumed Shiloh would have dealt with both.

"Yeah, Holsteins. Black and white mostly. They're a bunch of stubborn ladies, but they produce well and keep the farm afloat. I sell most of it, and I experiment with making cheese once in a while." He wasn't good at it, but it was something to do. "Nash spends his whole morning with them because I don't believe in those machines like the big farms have, you know?"

"Ah. That makes sense. Farm to table is a big deal these days, I know. You can make real money with organics and artisanal products." Wow, Shiloh could say many words all in a row.

"It is big," he agreed. "You know, a little farm stand or a table at the weekly farmer's market would be cool."

"Totally. You can grow dark greens over the winter—you'd have to heat the greenhouse, but it's doable." Shiloh grabbed a notepad out of his shirt pocket and started scribbling.

"Well, it's not frozen out there yet. We'd have some time to set that up. And in the spring, I mean...there's land for other stuff." *Stuff*...he shook his head. He knew nothing about growing anything. Not flowers, vegetables, nothing. He'd done months of research before trying cows and, in the beginning, it had been just a few. He was still trying to understand cheese.

"What are you interested in? Pretty? Useful? Medicinal? Food?" Shiloh dunked his doughnut and kept sketching and making notes.

He wasn't sure what he'd expected would happen when he made the offer in the bar, but he didn't think it would be this. The crinkly stress line in Shiloh's forehead was slowly disappearing, and that hooded look in the man's eyes was just...gone. "Whatever makes you happy?"

He blushed after he said it because that sounded way more personal than he'd intended, but that didn't make it any less true. He had no idea what he wanted; he just liked seeing Shiloh this relaxed.

"Well, if you're talking winter—I'd suggest a heated greenhouse with greens like mustard and mesclun, kale, cabbage, spinach. You could do peas and scallions. You can even start tomatoes and potatoes in the winter, if we protect them."

"Okay. It's up to you. But let me think about what I can

afford. I don't know what a greenhouse costs but it sounds like it would be a good investment." He'd kind of forgotten about the money when he suggested a greenhouse. Giving Shiloh some land wouldn't cost him anything, but this was getting a little more complicated now.

"Well, if you let me experiment, do some starts and all, I can put the greenhouse up. Just a little one so I can play and see what works and what doesn't."

"You can do whatever you like. Honestly. I'll see what I can do about getting you power for heat." And if it got too expensive, they'd talk about it. "It'll be nice having more people around out here. Nash is good company too."

"I've got some ideas for propane heat and wood heat. I've done a few situations with heater rocks as well. I'll put my brain to it."

"Wow. Sounds good to me." Tate put down his empty coffee cup. "You want to walk?"

"Sure. Sounds good." Shiloh stood and offered him a tentative smile. "Thanks for humoring me, man. I appreciate it."

That was an interesting word. "Humoring you? That makes it sound like I feel sorry for you or something."

"Well, I'd feel sorry for me if I did nothing but watch Food Network and sit at the bar."

He snorted and opened the door for Shiloh with a grin. "Well, you can feel sorry for yourself then."

"Fair enough." That earned him a low chuckle, and didn't that feel amazing, like he'd done something right.

It was a gorgeous day, still summer enough that the sun was warm, and the leaves weren't changing yet, but you could smell fall coming on the air. "So everything to the left of the barn and back that way is grazing land. Everything from the right of the barn over is just...wild. and there's some room behind the barn too that I mow just... I don't even know why. It looks nice." And it gave him somewhere to park extra cars when he needed to.

"Do you have a close personal relationship with your lawn mower?"

Wait. Was that a joke?

He glanced at Shiloh, straight-faced. "The nature of my relationship with my farm equipment is none of your business."

"Oh, I understand unique relationships, and I've heard some rumors about you farmers up here..."

"Oh, I'm not one of *those* farmers." He laughed. "I like how it looks. I mow it for no reason at all. I just like how it looks. And sometimes I'm bored and need to do something." He opened the door to the barn. "Everyone's healthy, and it's a nice day, so it's quiet in here right now."

"Healthy is good. I know how much it sucks to have sick livestock."

"Did you have horses? Bulls?" They wandered through the barn and out the back door.

"We had two hundred head of cattle, about five bucking futurity bulls, a half dozen horses."

"Really? And you gave that up? Wow. That sounds like it was quite an operation. Don't you miss it?" That wasn't a hobby, that was a business.

"I did give it up. It was Matty's, not mine."

That he could relate to. "I do understand a place not feeling like yours anymore." He steered them toward an open space far enough from the barn but still close enough to get to easily. "Over here maybe?"

"The cows won't be able to get to it, right?" Shiloh examined the ground, bending to check the soil. "I'd hate to lose a greenhouse because they smelled green food."

That was a smart question from a man that knew livestock. He watched Shiloh, finding himself interested in more than just what the man was doing. "If the fences hold they shouldn't, but probably the smart thing to do is fence it too. You know how they are. I had a few grazing in my front yard the other day." He could just imagine them trying to get into a warm greenhouse.

"I do know. It doesn't matter, does it? If they want through, they'll get through. Stubborn beasts. I've had them muscle into some odd damn spots." The soft chuckle read way more amused than frustrated.

"Sounds like a story you should tell me over a beer tonight." That came out differently than he'd intended, loaded maybe. And maybe it was, he couldn't even be sure himself right now. He liked Shiloh though, and they both knew damn well where they spent their Saturday nights.

"I don't like beer."

Was that growl embarrassment? Aggravation? Amusement? Tate crossed his arms. "Oh? Fine. Pizza."

"Pizza I like. Whiskey is fine too. No beer. Also, no pineapple on the pizza. That's a crime against nature."

"So judgy." He liked pineapple on pizza. He liked anchovies on pizza too. Hamburger, buffalo chicken, pesto, broccoli...he was in. "Pizza inspires creativity."

"I used to make one with salsa, goat cheese, and chicken..."

"Yeah? I'd eat that. It sounds good. Fancy too." He led Shiloh a little deeper into the property so he could get a feel for it.

"I used to cook more. No reason now."

Oh no. Don't go all dark and low again. He liked that smile.

"No reason? If you enjoy it find a reason! Go cook for

your friends...they have kids, right? You can cook for the fundraiser at school next month. You can cook for me."

Shiloh blinked at him. "There's a fundraiser? How do you know?"

"I teach at the high school. There's a fundraising dinner for the soccer team."

"Oh." Shiloh seemed utterly confused for a second, then he just shook his head. "I probably shouldn't start back up with something like that."

"Start back up...?" Now he was the one that was confused.

"Well, it's been a few years. What if I suck now?"

"Is that something you forget? You can forget how to cook? Seems like it's either something you can do, or you can't. And anyway, how do you know unless you try?" Shiloh was like this heavy stone sitting at the top of a hill, and Tate was just shoving it, and nudging and poking at it, trying to make it start to roll on its own.

"I have no idea. I mean, maybe? I assume you lose the physical skills, but what do I know?" There was that almost smile again, and Tate thought he could see Shiloh's tension ease the longer he was out here.

He shrugged. "I make a few easy dinners for one, so I am not the one to answer that question. You want to make pizza here instead of going out? I'm sure there's a game on." There was always a game on, right?

"I—" Shiloh stopped and blinked. "I suppose we could. Sure. I don't see why not. You don't have other plans?"

He wasn't sure why he was so invested in Shiloh, but he loved the way things he said seemed to surprise the cowboy so much. "It's just me and my cows out here. And the bar can wait a night."

"I don't know about that." At his curious look, Shiloh

tilted his head. "Well, I've not missed a night. There's no proof the bar can survive me missing one. It may interrupt some massive space-time continuum thing."

He grinned. This was so much better. "That was funny! The cowboy has a sense of humor. I love it."

"Just keep it between us. It's sort of a secret." The words were delivered in a perfect deadpan—good enough that if he hadn't had the wink, he might not have known Shiloh was teasing.

He shook his head. "My lips are sealed, man. I'm not one to out anyone." If he'd known Shiloh just a little better, he'd have given the man a playful shove, but he was keeping his hands to himself for now. Shiloh still seemed pretty unpredictable and this new trust between them felt fragile.

"Dude." Shiloh stopped short. They were at a little thicket of trees with vines trailing along the ground at the edges, and Shiloh studied them carefully, ignoring the thorns. "Look at this!"

"Wow! It's green!" He shrugged. "I'm sorry. I don't know what I'm looking at."

"*Rubus vermontanus*, I think. These little stalked glands on the base of the flower stem say it is. Those are rare. I love blackberries."

"Vermontanus? You made that up." He didn't spend much time on this side of the property, but Shiloh had to be pulling his leg.

Tate got a *look*, then Shiloh pulled out his phone, typing furiously for a second before showing him a website that said "Rubus vermontanus" at the top.

"You're not. Wow." He'd never heard of it. But then again, he wasn't exactly a farmer, or a botanist, or even interested much in plants. If it was in a salad, he ate it. "That cool. Still you have to admit, Vermont-anus sounds like you made it up."

Shiloh stared at him long enough that he thought he'd really pissed the man off, then the laughter started, hard and loud, rocking the man's whole body.

He watched Shiloh laughing, listened to how free it sounded, and laughed along in relief. "You see what I mean? Stupid name for a plant, right?"

"You can totally tell that you work around teenagers, man. Completely." Shiloh was...so much younger than Tate had thought. Look at those dark eyes shine.

He nodded. "Oh, deep down? I'm a twelve-year-old boy. Absolutely. I'm not above jokes involving bodily functions or stupid puns or dad jokes either."

"So, fart jokes are a go. Got it." Shiloh's lips twitched.

"Oh, yeah. Bring it." He nodded solemnly. Shiloh had just been laughing hard, so by all rights he should have broken first, but Tate's composure was hanging by a thread and after a second he didn't even fight it. He snorted like a pig and doubled over giggling.

"Oh, Jesus fuck..." Shiloh lost it, just plopping down on the grass and laughing like a loon.

"Oh, man," he said, still giggling and gulping air. "You made me snort. That was...so *suave*."

"Soignee, right? Isn't that supposed to mean classy and shit?"

"Soi..." He stared down at Shiloh. "It must be classy because I have no idea what you're talking about."

"They say it on the Food Network. It sounds fancy." Shiloh shook his head at them both. "Look at us, man, laughing in the grass."

He straightened and offered Shiloh a hand up.

"Laughter is good for you. And you're way more handsome when you laugh too."

"I haven't had a lot of reasons lately, so thanks. I may have lost a couple three brain cells I laughed so hard."

He noted for future reference that Shiloh ignored his compliment but didn't remark on it. "You won't miss them. I mean, you're going to be talking to plants." He hauled Shiloh to his feet.

"True, but I got to tell you, it's when they start talking back that you got yourself a problem." Shiloh brushed his butt off.

The dad joke, or close enough, was adorable. "It's that way with most things. Even my students."

"Do you like it? Teaching? I don't think I'd be too good at it, to be honest."

"I love it. I love math, it's useful and fascinating, and I love trying to get kids to see what I see." He loved math, and he also really liked people. "Also, I just happen to think teenagers are pretty cool. They're moody sometimes, hormonal, sure, but they're in this space between being a kid and being an adult and trying to learn who they are... I love to listen to them talk, hear what they're into. They're as interesting as math."

"Well, good on you, man. Teachers are necessary as all get out. Me? I'm into growing shit." Shiloh didn't sound like he was blowing smoke.

He smiled because it was nice to be appreciated. "Food is kind of important too, you know." They climbed the front steps and back onto the porch.

"A little bit, yeah? Starvation is no one's friend." Shiloh stopped at the top step. "I got to be honest, I'm not clear on what I'm supposed to do next. Do you want me to come back tonight? What do you want me to bring?"

He felt that too, the awkwardness. He wasn't sure what to do about it. "Well, I guess if we're cooking we better...shop?"

"Want to go together?" Shiloh seemed surprised that he asked.

"Why not? Sure. Let me get my keys." Yeah, this was awkward. They barely knew each other, and he'd made this impulsive invitation, and now they had hours to kill between now and anything resembling a reasonable dinner time.

Then again, Shiloh seemed like he was enjoying the company so...

So they were going shopping.

7

S hiloh had never had a weirder afternoon, and he'd been shopping with the bullfighters' wives.

They'd shopped for seeds, wine, and groceries. They'd driven around and looked at other greenhouses. They'd even stopped at a coffee shop and played a game of cribbage.

Weird.

But not bad.

Now they were back at Tate's place, and they were unloading the groceries.

"I'm going to put on some music." Tate ducked into the living room and put on something he didn't recognize. "It's getting dark earlier these days, have you noticed?"

"I have, believe it or not." He looked up his recipe for pizza dough on his phone and started blooming the yeast.

Tate snorted. "Okay, okay. I didn't mean that as a hermit joke. So sensitive." Tate gave him a goofy cross-eyed look and stuck out his tongue.

"That'll earn you detention, teach." He found himself

beginning to tease, to relax. It was harder than he had imagined.

"With you? I'll take it." Tate pulled the wine out of a bag and opened it. "Ready for a glass?"

"Sure. Thanks for going with a dry for me." He knew enough about wine to know what he liked, and he liked them dryer than not.

He rolled his eyes at himself. He was being a dipshit. Seriously.

"Honestly, I don't know a dry from a...well, something else." Tate was pretty good at opening a bottle though. "Thanks for not making me drink whiskey all night."

"No. Neither one of us needs that. I only ever have one."

"One? You sit there all night with one glass? God, I'd be so sick of listening to myself think. How do you do that?" The wine glasses Tate produced were stemless and sturdy looking.

"I'm—Shit, man, I've just been listening to my own damn brain." And that was the truth. He'd been wallowing.

"You must have one very interesting brain." Tate poured two glasses of wine and handed him one. "Here's to... growing something amazing."

He lifted his glass. "Here's to a new—friendship."

"And a new friendship." Tate's smile, so easy and genuine, lit up the kitchen for a second before it was covered by a wine glass.

"Yeah." He sipped, and the wine just was perfect. He thought that Sky would be tickled that he was here, making pizza, and talking to Tate.

"So put me to work. What do you need me to do? Chop something? Stir something? Stay the hell out of your way?"

"The pizza dough has to rest and then rise. Did you want

to make that grilling cheese to have as an app?" He loved that stuff, and Tate had been more than willing to try it.

"Oh, yeah. Let's do that. There is no bad with cheese, right?" Tate pulled it out of the shopping bag. "Hall-oooo-mi. Is that right? Halloumi? I'll get the grill pan going."

"Halloumi, yeah. I've had it with jalapeno, bacon, Italian seasoning, chipotle." He loved it, and he tended to have it fairly regularly.

"Well, I can grill I think." Tate wrestled the package open and turned up the heat in his grill pan. "This might be the most complicated thing ever made in my kitchen."

"It's easy. I swear. Just oil and warm up your grill pan." He loved the way it was melty and grilled at the same time.

"Okay. I can handle that." Tate drizzled some oil. "Where did you learn to cook?"

"I like to eat, and Matt was not going to cook anything—nothing at all. So if I didn't want to eat fast food burgers and Walmart fried chicken for every meal? I had to learn."

"I like your survival instinct. I eat out a lot. Or make eggs. Or grilled cheese sandwiches." Tate set the cheese on the grill pan. "Speaking of..."

"Just let it sit for a few minutes. Don't move it."

"Don't move it." Tate put his hands up in the air and stepped back from the stove, then picked up his wine. "Not touching. This is a good time for a sip."

"Totally. Sip away." He was going by his nose. The scent of cooking cheese was like heaven, and he'd learned exactly when to turn it.

Tate watched him. "You're good with a knife. You look like a pro."

"I've been doing it for a while, I guess." And it felt good. Damn good.

"Oh, I love this song." Tate started swaying to Kane

Brown and dancing with his wine glass. "You know this guy? He gets tons of airplay up here."

"I do, yeah. I love his music. He really respects the genre." He hummed along until he smelled the cheese. "Turn it, man."

Tate spun in a circle. "Oh...did you mean the cheese? On it." He got a wink and then Tate used a large spatula to turn the cheese over. "Ooh pretty. It smells amazing."

"And see? You let it get done right, it don't stick."

"I can't say I wasn't skeptical, but you've won me over." Tate poured himself another glass of wine. "You really can nurse a drink. You have a lot of wine left in that glass."

"I do, don't I?" He could probably manage two without worrying about driving home, so he took another deep drink, humming as it hit his tongue.

"That's better." Tate peered over at the stove. "How do we know it's done?"

"Give it one more minute and then we'll pull it. The dough's ready. It just needs to rest."

"Okay, what else can I do?" Tate struck a pose with his wine glass. "I can probably do more than just drink wine and look pretty."

"You want to get some crackers and sit and snack?" If they were eating, he could shove food in his mouth instead of making small talk. The little now-brown block of cheese was perfect for two people.

"I can do that." Tate moved behind him and pulled the crackers they'd bought out of the shopping bag. "Pull it off now?"

"Yep." The cheese came off with a perfect crust.

"That is cool. It smells so good." Tate set it on a plate, opened the crackers and sat on a tall stool at the kitchen island.

Shiloh cut the crust because they wanted to eat the melty part first, then the crispy crust. Then he took a deep sip of his wine. Perfect.

The look in Tate's eyes was full of heat when he glanced up, but it disappeared as soon as their eyes met. Tate sipped his wine quickly and cleared his throat. "The wine is good, huh?"

"It is. I am addicted to this stuff." He licked his lips clean, tasting drops of the wine.

"Addicted to wine? I think there's a program for that." Tate winked and took a bite of the cheese on a cracker. "Oh, mmm. So good."

"Are you calling me a wino?" He cracked up, knowing that wasn't what Tate meant.

"Well, no. But if it'll keep you smiling like that, I might." Tate set his wine down and grabbed another bite of cheese.

He took a piece for himself, and it tasted damn good. Cheese was a thing all on its own—funky and creamy and unique.

"Hm." Tate made a thoughtful sound as he finished his wine. "Guess we should get to making the pizza."

"Oh. Sure. Absolutely." God, he had become a boring old dude. "Let me check the dough. If it's not ready, I'll try and encourage it to rise."

"Oh, dirty talk. I like it."

Shiloh blinked, and then the laughter just bubbled up out of him.

"That laugh, though." Tate just shook his head and refilled his glass. "More wine?"

"Yeah, yes, I think I will, thank you." More wine, more laughter. More of all of it.

Tate topped him off, not in the bartender glass half full way, but the right on up to the top way. "So. A grasshopper walks into a bar..." Tate glanced at him. "Stop me if you know this one."

He chuckled, tilted his head, and said, "You have a drink named Steve?"

Tate blushed and rolled his eyes. "That's the one. I'm awful at jokes."

"Really? I bet you hear them from your students. Dad jokes?" Surely that was a thing. He'd heard every fucking bar joke there was, and don't even get him started on the cowboy jokes. Christ. Hawk Destry thought he was a goddamn comedian.

Oh, dad jokes. "It's so cheap to throw a party in a haunted house. The ghosts bring all the boos." Tate grinned and sipped his wine.

Okay, that was funny. "Uh...did you know what Forrest Gump's password is? One-Forrest-one."

"Oh, man. That's enough of that." Tate peered around him at the pizza dough. "Well?"

"I think it'll do." It wasn't great, but he thought Tate was ready for him to eat and get out of his hair. He would normally let it go another hour or so, but that didn't matter.

"I'm sorry, I'm just hungry." Tate stood close beside him. Close enough for him to get a whiff of aftershave. "And not patient. In case you hadn't noticed. There's a reason I work with teenagers... I share their short attention span."

"Well, I will feed you." He worked with the dough as little as possible and cranked up Tate's oven to 550. He worked quickly and did his best not to make a mess.

"So when do you want to get started on the greenhouse? You can work out here any time you want; Nash will be here, the house will be open, even if I'm at school."

He was going to have to work this out in his head, but he had a better idea than he'd started with. "Let me do some research. How long do I have before it's too cold to put posts in the ground?"

"Maybe a month? We'll get our first frost any day now, and then it's only a few weeks before we're cold."

"Okay, maybe by next weekend, then. I want to set everything up and get growing." He was excited about the prospect, though.

"Good. The weekend. Then I can help. Not Nash though; he takes most weekends off. You can buy whatever you need ahead of time and store it in the barn. Big empty stall right as you walk in on the right."

"And you'll warn your man?" He didn't want to get shot.

"I will warn Nash. But he's not that type...if you said, 'Hey Tate said I could', he'd just believe you and go about his business." Tate peered at him, teasing. "He might not let you in the house to pee though."

"Good to know. I do know how to piss in the woods, so that's handy."

"Of course you do. You're a cowboy at heart." Tate stuffed another cheese-covered cracker in his mouth.

He didn't know. He'd known so many cowboys that he didn't think of himself as one, but it was nice to hear.

"Maybe we should make a little party out of putting up the greenhouse on Saturday. You could invite your friends from the bar, and I'll invite a few too. You know what they say about many hands, right? We could have a cookout. What do you think?"

"Oh, I only know Sky and Beck, and they have children. Three of them. Very active ones." Charlie was stunning, but that little girl was damn intense and mad at him to boot.

"So invite them." Tate shrugged like he hadn't heard a word he'd just said.

"I'll ask." But he couldn't imagine dealing with them and

power tools and dirt and cows. Although, they were half cowboy... "But, regardless, I can help provide whatever for your meal."

Tate blinked at him. "*Our* meal. It's our cookout, for your greenhouse."

"Okay, then I totally will provide the food. What's your position on brisket?" He didn't have a smoker, but he could make one on a grill or even in a roaster. Damn, he missed having a smoker. He could so smoke a brisket...

"I've never had one. I've had steaks..."

He stopped. Stared. That was... Poor neglected man. That was obscene. "You're not serious. Maybe I can set a smoker up behind the bar..."

"A smoker?"

Could Tate seriously not know what a smoker was?

"You know, you smoke meat? Like ribs and all? Smoked turkey?" It was a thing. It really was.

"Oh! Sorry, I grew up under a rock I guess. You want a smoker, just set it up here." Tate gave him a wink. "I mean... if you're planning on cooking."

"I am, but... Okay, a brisket takes twelve to fifteen hours of watching. You mind if I'm here that long?" He could wait in his truck, but that seemed...extreme.

"If you're serious about bringing a smoker and doing all that work? Hell yes. It sounds like fun. And a great reward for spending all day working our butts off."

Oh. Okay. That was unexpected, but also? Welcome. Honestly. "Well, then, I'll come over Friday evening and start it. I'll put the rub on it Thursday so it can do its work."

"It's a date!" Tate held up his wine glass like it was a toast, so he followed along and clinked their glasses together.

"Works for me." He took a sip and then slipped the pizza in the oven. "Give it about ten minutes."

"I'll go see what's on TV." Tate took his wine and disappeared into the living room.

He set a timer on his phone, then followed Tate. "Do you have to milk your cows, or does your man do it?"

"Nash, usually. He kind of fell into it. He needed work, and I needed more time to grade papers. He's kind of a fixture now, and he does other things as I need them. Repairing fences, mucking, whatever. I sell almost all the milk."

"That's amazing. You said you make cheese too?" That idea sort of made him happy.

"I try?" Tate grinned. "I haven't quite succeeded."

"I—You want to discuss your recipes? We can talk about it over the pizza?" He found himself smiling back, which he hadn't done so much, in a long, long time.

"Oh, I'm supposed to have a recipe?" Tate tilted his head. "Kidding! Yeah, I can tell you what I do, I don't know. I've only tried a couple things."

"Excellent. I'm... I'm in." The timer for the pizza went off, and he was... In.

8

Tate was obsessed with this new greenhouse idea. He wasn't losing sleep over it, but he was definitely conjuring up pictures in his mind and daydreaming about his land being put to good use. Shiloh though...thoughts about that man were keeping him up at night.

Shiloh had been sitting in the corner of the bar for a month at least, keeping to himself, nursing a whiskey, having no interest at all in anyone, but Saturday night in Tate's kitchen the man smiled and made jokes, cooked and shared a bottle of wine like he wanted to be there.

And completely ignored every overture Tate had made.

Tate had even told him to bring over a smoker. He'd never even seen a smoker. Did he want one in his backyard? It didn't matter, he wanted Shiloh there, and if a smoker did the trick, he'd let anyone set one up.

Tate set his coffee down in the faculty room and sat with it. He was early as usual, but it seemed like he needed that coffee more than most days because he barely remembered his drive to work this morning. He needed to clear his head before he walked into a room full of tenth graders.

Bryn came wandering in, looking exactly like the cheerleaders she coached—a bright light, perfectly made up, hair in a ponytail, latte in hand. "Morning, Tate. How goes life?"

He grinned because this was Vermont, but you couldn't take Boston out of the girl. "Oh, fine. Fine. Busy. I have... things going on." That was ridiculous. He never had things going on.

"Ooh, things? I like things. Talk." She sat down and offered him a doughnut. "I brought two, I'll share."

"I will take you up on that." He took a piece of a glazed doughnut, popped it in his mouth, and then licked his sticky fingers. "I met a guy. It's complicated, but he's a little older; he lost his husband a couple of years ago...but I like him."

"Oh. So, what's the problem? Is he not nice to you?"

Now that was the question, wasn't it? What was the problem?

"Me, I think?" He shrugged. "He was nice, we laughed, and he smiled a lot—he has such a great smile—but he's just not interested in me. Like, at all. And I guess I can respect that, but I mean, he didn't reject me either. It was weird."

"Well, is he clear on what you're doing? It's been a while since he's been...on the market."

"He's a man, isn't he? How can he not—" He frowned. "Well, that's a thought, actually." He'd flirted, smiled back, made some on-the-edge jokes...and Shiloh had smiled and gone right on making pizza.

Maybe Shiloh had been flirting back too, he just was unused to the game. Hell, Tate had no idea how cowboys flirted...maybe it was with beer and hat tipping.

And he hadn't had a beer or a hat.

"Mhm. His heart is broken. Maybe you need to push a little."

Well, shit. He hadn't thought about that either. "Or back off."

"Or that. Did you get that vibe?"

"I...got no vibe. Zero vibe. He was vibeless."

Bryn laughed in that way she did, filling the entire faculty room with the sound. Everyone glanced their direction and he gave a goofy little wave, which made most people grin and go back to their business. "I imagine it's hard to put yourself out there. Where does he work?"

He shook his head. "He doesn't."

"He doesn't work?"

He shrugged. "He hangs out at my local bar..."

"Run. People need to work. You don't need a deadbeat drunk." She shook her head. "Danger, Will Robinson."

He frowned. Shiloh wasn't a drunk, was he? He said he sat there with the same whiskey all night at the bar. The two of them had barely finished that bottle of wine—and most of that he'd drunk himself. "You don't think maybe he just needs a push? I'm giving him some space for a greenhouse; he's a gardener or a botanist or something. I mean, he lost the love of his life, you know? And he has friends. Local friends with kids and stuff."

"A botanist? Did you say he was local?" She nibbled at her donut like the secrets of the world were in there.

"No, he's from Texas I think." This conversation was so strange, he felt like his fascination with Shiloh was totally normal, but saying it all out loud made it seem so weird. "I'm not exactly sure how he ended up in Vermont. It does seem like a hike, huh?"

"From Texas? God yes. Maybe he just needed

somewhere totally new. You said he has friends here, though."

"He does. You know that guy that runs that rodeo up here every spring? Shiloh is friends with him. So I guess he has a reason to be up here, and I don't think he's been here all that long." He shrugged. "I guess he probably needs some time."

"Well, maybe you should just ask. Some people like that. Directness and everything."

"Hey, Shiloh, are you into me? Because you're a hot cowboy." He laughed and waggled his eyebrows. "That direct?"

"Why not?" She shrugged one shoulder. "Or you could say, 'Hey, nice boots. Wanna?'"

He laughed. "Is that how you do it?"

"It works for me." She winked, but her face turned serious then. "Listen, just be honest. If he's not interested, then you can be friends. If he is, then you know."

Yeah, maybe. He didn't want to make things weird. If he said something and Shiloh was totally not interested, could they really just be friends after that? "I'm having a cookout on Saturday if you're interested. Shiloh is smoking a brisket, which is apparently a Texas thing." He chuckled. "And we're putting up the greenhouse."

"Wow. Wow, okay. Well, maybe. Sure. Why not?" She chuckled. "Can I bring someone, and what should I bring to share?"

"Bring anyone you want. And um... I don't know. Dessert?" He was going to invite all his bar friends too, and hopefully Shiloh's buddies would find a babysitter but if not, well...they'd corral the kiddos somehow.

"Cool. Thanks for the invitation. It sounds like fun." She

squeezed his hand. "Talk to him. I mean, if that doesn't work, if he gets mad, he sucks."

"Right." He nodded as the bell rang and stood up. Time to be a teacher. "Thank you. You're right."

Hopefully.

He'd think about it.

9

Shiloh went bouncing along the road to Tate's dairy. He had a huge smoker, two briskets, a ham, a shitton of potatoes and cabbage, beer, wood chips, and a change of clothes for tomorrow. Also, everything he needed for pancakes in the morning.

Contrary to Tate's account of things, it wasn't hard to find a smoker, and plenty of folks had heard of them or had one in their own yard. But Tate didn't seem to cook much, so he wasn't surprised. He was ready to relax and have some fun, get his greenhouse up, and show off his cooking skills. It had been a long while since he'd entertained.

His excitement worried him a little bit, but that was fading, if he was honest. It was easier to have something to look forward to—both the greenhouse and the party.

And the guy.

"Just shut up." What did he know about dating now? Nothing. At all. He would just fuck it up.

Plus, Tate had a lot of friends, and from what he'd seen, Tate didn't seem to want a piece of any of them. Maybe Tate was taken. Or married to his job. Or celibate.

That happened. People were celibate. Hell, he was damn near a virgin again, right?

He snorted. People were not celibate. Not guys like Tate. Men like Tate were looking for just the right guy.

He was not the right guy for a barely thirty-year-old school teacher.

He turned into Tate's driveway, and a big blond guy waved him down and gestured for him to roll down his window. "Hey. Are you Shiloh?"

"Yes, sir. Shiloh Williams. I brought the smoker."

"Cool. I'm Nash, Tate said to drive around back to set up your smoker. I'm here to help." Nash pointed to where the driveway disappeared around the front porch.

"Oh, cool. Nice to meet you, man. Seriously. This smoker is heavy as hell." He pulled around and parked, hopping out to start unloading.

Nash jogged around the house to join him. "Tate had to do a delivery after school, but he'll be here soon." Nash grinned at him. "I'm stronger than he is anyway. Just tell me where you need me."

"I'm going to move this bad boy down to the tailgate, then we'll work together to get it to the ground?" That seemed like the best way to not kill either one of them.

"Works for me." Nash waited for him and with some grunting and negotiating, the two of them managed to get it off the truck. "More awkward than heavy." Nash glanced sideways at him and grinned. "That's bullshit. That thing is heavy as fuck."

"No shit on that. We'll put it next to his grill. He does have a grill, doesn't he?" Everyone had a grill.

"It's dusty, but he has one." Nash pointed to a little brick patio at the back of the house. "I've never seen him use it. So what's the plan here?"

"We'll set them up together. I might get them both going tomorrow." He dragged the smoker over, making an L with it and the grill.

"Fancy fancy. Tate said something about brisket?" Nash closed up his tailgate for him and clapped the dust off his hands.

"Two briskets and a ham. Parties need a lot of good food."

"Mm. Ham. That works. I guess Tate has a whole crew coming tomorrow. Should be fun. He even invited me." Nash laughed. "He's never had a party here I don't think."

"No? Well, we can do it up nice, right?" Surely Nash was wrong. Tate was young. Decent. Involved in the community.

"For sure. This looks like a good setup. What else can I —oh, and there he is."

Tate wandered around the side of the house wearing blue jeans and a big smile. "Hey! Look at that. Sorry I'm late." Tate offered a hand to shake. "Looks like Nash is getting you settled in."

"That's what you pay me for." Nash stepped out of the way.

He shook, then tried his best to figure out whether or not he was messing up something for Nash and Tate by being here.

"I do some microbrewery deliveries after school a few days a week. Fridays are a big day, and I didn't want you to show up to an empty house."

"Yeah, bullshit. You didn't want to muscle that smoker off his truck."

Tate grinned. "I'm scrawny compared to him."

"Well, we got it down, and I appreciate it muchly." He nodded and smiled, keeping it friendly.

"Come on, Nash, I've got your pay in my truck."

"Yup. Gotta go blow it on my date."

Tate glanced at him. "His date could be one of my students."

"Liar! He's twenty." Nash laughed.

"Oh, you're cradle-robbing!" Shiloh had to tease. Had to, because he'd been that nineteen-year-old kid, staring up a cowboy and being dry-mouthed.

"He's got a big boy bed, I swear!"

"Yeah, yeah. Come on, let me pay you so you can...do whatever you do with a twenty-year-old."

"Well, if you don't know..."

"Ugh!" Tate groaned. "Be right back." Tate winked at him and hustled Nash into the house through the back door.

He started hauling in food—the meat had been in the dry rub for a day, so it would be ready to pop in soon, and the rest was easy to bring in and put away.

Tate came back a few minutes later and pulled a beer out of the fridge. "That smoker looks pretty sweet; you'll have to show me how it works. You want something to drink? A soda? Wine? I have some harder stuff in that cabinet up there."

"I've got a Coke right now." He held up his Dr Pepper bottle. "But I might put a shot in it later. I brought turkey subs for supper."

"Oh, nice. I was thinking about ordering pizza so you beat me to it. Thank you. How long does the meat stay in the smoker?"

"Fifteen to eighteen hours on the brisket. Twelve on the ham, but they will be done in plenty of time." It didn't take a lot of work, just a lot of time.

"That's amazing. You want to go eat out back? It's a tiny bit chilly, but the porch has a great view of the sunset."

"Sounds great. I'll get the smoker set up after." He handed over a turkey, bacon, avocado. Those were the best.

"Come on. I want to hear about your week." Tate tucked the sub under one arm and took his hand—*took his hand*—to lead him out to the porch.

He followed, his tongue lacquered to the top of his mouth, excitement making the pit of his belly hot.

There was a nice setup there, a wrought iron table and a couple of matching chairs. Very intricate work, painted white. Tate pulled out his chair. "They're prettier than they are comfortable, but they were one of the few things that survived the fire."

"They're good. I used to have Adirondack chairs at our place. They're comfortable unless they're wet."

"They're pretty common up here. I bet you could find some." Tate sat too and opened up his sandwich, eyes on him like he was actually interested. "So, there's a lot of stuff in my barn. You had a busy week, huh?"

"I did. I have blueprints and supplies, food and folks to help." And it had been entertaining. He hadn't realized how bored he'd been.

"It's going to be quite a party tomorrow then. I guess it's time I had some people here for something. I'm glad we decided to do this." Tate smiled at him. "You're overdue for some fun I think, cowboy."

"Yeah? What about you? Are you ready for some of that fun?" He found Tate a grin, let it sit on his face.

"I'm always ready for some." Tate's head tilted and he got a wink.

"Ha!" He leaned back, eyes on the sunset. "Wow. This is fine. Nash said you were making a delivery?"

"My second job. I drive a truck for Proud Dog, the microbrewery? I deliver to a bunch of bars after school."

"So you work three jobs? Shit, man..." He thought that being a teacher was enough. That was intense work.

"Gotta pay the bills. And I'm saving for a truck. And I want horses." Tate grinned, looking proud. "This is going to be a functioning farm one day. Self-sustaining."

"I can see that. Seriously." That was the big dream, wasn't it? Being able to have a piece of land that worked, that made its money back.

"We'll see. I'm still learning, so I'm socking away some cash in the meantime. It's not like I have a life." Tate snorted and touched his hand again with warm, steady fingers. "This sandwich is good. Thank you."

"You're more than welcome." Damn, he was getting goosebumps.

"It's good to have you back here, away from the bar, where it's quieter. Where we can talk. You know? The other night I really felt like we were...connecting."

"I hear you." And he did, honestly. This was infinitely better than the bar. "I enjoyed chatting with you, cooking together. It made the bar feel lonely."

Oh god. Shut. Up.

Tate seemed to understand what he was saying. "That's a funny thing, right? How you can still feel lonely in a crowd. Do you feel that way when you're nursing that whiskey in your booth?"

"Sometimes. I do a lot of people watching." And he talked to himself. A lot.

"Yeah? I guess you watch my crazy crew playing pool and darts and trying not to get too drunk on a school night, huh? Do you ever...watch anyone in particular?" Tate had given up on his sandwich and those deep blue eyes were trained on him.

"There's this one guy—he always makes me feel like he

sees me when he walks by to hit the head..." He held Tate's gaze, letting the man see.

Tate nodded, slowly closing the space between them. "You should get to know him better. I think he likes you."

"I hope so. I'm sort of spending the night at his house..." And he didn't know what to think about it, but he was here.

"Yeah. I'm thinking we better start slow." Tate's lips hovered close for a second, then brushed against his. "Real slow." Tate meant what he'd said. The first touch of their lips was gentle, testing, but not at all shy. The second more purposeful, but Tate was still offering, and seemed to be waiting for his response. "Seems like a good call to me."

"It does." He dared to press their lips together, his heart racing wildly. Oh. Tate's mouth was so soft.

Tate hummed and slid from the chair right into his lap, one arm sliding around his shoulders. "Yeah," Tate whispered as they took a breath, then came back for more. He remembered this, being so present that there was no hurry, no end game, just time with each other.

Tate didn't push it, and Shiloh felt like he could be here, right here, and okay at the same time. He fed on the kisses, each one like a...a...a sip of coffee with sweet whipped cream on top.

The kiss ended naturally after a while and Tate leaned back enough that he could see the smile. "I've been looking forward to that."

"Have you? I wasn't... I wasn't sure if you were... I mean, I'm an old dude." And Tate was pretty.

Tate snorted. "Seriously? I thought we were clicking pretty well the other night, but you were giving me nothing. That's all I've thought about all week."

His cheeks went red-hot, and he shrugged. He wasn't

used to this. He wasn't absolutely sure he was ready to re-enter life. But he was here, wasn't he?

"Hey." Tate kissed his forehead and slid back off his lap into his own chair, taking his hand instead. "Slow is okay with me. And I'm not just saying that to be nice or whatever. It's fine. And if you're not—" Tate snorted and shook his head. "I was about to say if you're not really into this that's okay too, but I don't think I'm going to let you off that easy."

"I'm not a liar. I'm rusty, but not dead." He imagined, unless Tate was stupid, that they were both aware that they both did it for each other.

"You're definitely not dead. You're much too warm to be dead. And too handsome." Tate winked at him. "How about we set up that smoker and...see how things go after that?"

"Sounds like a plan. Don't forget your sandwich." He stood and started hooking up the propane tank. "I put the legs and such on last night. So, I went with propane—it's a better flavor than electric, fewer headaches than charcoal, safer than pellets."

"If you say so. I'm kind of grill-clueless." Tate left their sandwiches right where they were. "But you know, I learn fast. And I am totally capable of calculating the ratio of weight to temperature to time for you." Tate clucked his tongue. "Because you know, math teacher."

"Excellent. That's the hard part. I'm a grill guy, I admit. I love cooking outside." Shiloh got the grates set up. "I got two briskets and a ham. I'm thinking the ham on top, the briskets toward the bottom. The beef will go in first."

"So am I the ham or the brisket?" Tate winked at him and didn't even blush.

"You mean we can't be ribs? Turkey?" Did that even make sense? "And if you're asking, I like both pitching and catching. I also do hand jobs, oral, rubbing wildly and calling it dancing..."

Tate's jaw dropped almost comically, and then he broke out into wild laughter. "Jesus Christ, thank you for the resume..." Tate giggled himself backward a couple of steps.

"Hey, you asked, Sunshine. I was just being honest."

"No no, I like honest." Tate gasped, trying to straighten up. "I do. I love it. That was just the very last thing I would have expected to come out of your mouth. I mean, after that super-hot, but super chaste kiss, and last week's barely meeting my eyes over a whole bottle of wine." Tate moved closer, a simple, happy look on his face. "Here I was being so careful..."

"Were you?" God, that was so sweet. Seriously. It was absolutely dear, and Shiloh was honored. "Thank you."

"I was. I am. I don't know what it's like to be you, you know? I don't want to scare you off being too...me. Too forward."

"I don't know how to be me either, believe it or not. I've never dated as a widower before. I feel like I don't know how." Look at him, going for brutal honestly.

"So we're both clueless but well-intentioned." Tate still hadn't lost that smile. "Cool. We can work with that."

"We can. You want to grab me one of the briskets? We'll put them on first, then the ham in a few hours."

"They're in the cooler?" Tate tugged the lid open. "Wow, there's a lot of meat in here."

They got the meat in, the wood chips in the smoke box, the fire set, and the door locked. "Now I need to add chips once an hour or so. And that's that."

Now they just had to occupy themselves for hours and hours.

"Wow. You really know what you're doing. That's so cool. People are going to be so impressed tomorrow."

"We'll see. If Sky is, that'll do. He's a picky son of a bitch." He winked, proving he was teasing.

"He texted me; you must have given him my number? He's bringing the kids for like five minutes so they can see you and then their nanny is picking them up."

"Does that seem weird to you? Having a nanny?" It did to him. He couldn't imagine it. Sky was the only person he knew that had one.

Tate shrugged. "I don't know. How many kids do they have? Are they working? Do they travel for work? People need to do what they need to do right?"

"Totally! I'm not being evil." He just didn't remember hearing that outside of Mary Poppins or wealthy couples. It just seemed...fascinating.

Tate popped him on the shoulder. "I didn't mean that. I don't know. I work with kids; they have all kinds of family situations. But I heard Sky was champ, so I bet he's sitting on some cash."

"Oh, he was. He was amazing. My—Matty idolized him. Said he was the best in the business."

"Wow. Maybe I can find a ride on YouTube. I know he's pretty damn popular up here when that bull riding thing he sponsors comes around."

"He is. Folks care about him a lot. I've got a bunch of rides saved. I'll dig some up." He had videos of the great ones and every one of Matty's rides.

"Oh that would be cool. Come on, let's go sit. You want a drink?" Tate's fingers slid against his palm.

"I do. And I want the rest of my supper." He curled their fingers together, squeezed.

"Hungry man." Tate tugged him over to the table and sat him down. "You eat. What can I get you? You want that shot for your Dr Pepper?"

"You know what, Sunshine? I think that sounds great." This smile felt more natural. In fact, it felt real.

10

Tate pulled the whiskey down from a high shelf and dusted the bottle off. It had been a while since he'd opened it, obviously, but it still smelled good.

He couldn't help his grin thinking about Shiloh as he grabbed another beer for himself. Every moment had been better than the one before it. Shiloh was funny, he was smart, interesting, hotter by the minute and that kiss...

That kiss.

Tate hadn't made a first move in his whole life. And he'd never expected to be rewarded with...that. Wow. Slow, patient, but tinged with promise.

Knowing smiles barely acknowledging that they had a whole long night ahead of them.

Just...wow.

He opened his beer and headed back to the porch with it in one hand and the whiskey in the other.

Shiloh was sitting, face up toward the sky, humming softly, and Tate thought he'd never looked more beautiful. Still and strong and gorgeous. He hung out in the doorway just watching for a second before asking, "What are you humming?"

"Hmm? Oh, just some lullaby I barely remember. My granny used to sing all the time." Shiloh chuckled, and the sound was warm, happy.

"Are you going to sing me to sleep?" He set the whiskey down on the table, then touched Shiloh's arm, drawing his fingers from one shoulder to the other.

"Mmm... Maybe. After a bunch more of them kisses." Oh, Shiloh's drawl got heavy when he was turned on. Good to know.

That drawl gave him goosebumps, but those words made his heart race. It tapped against his ribs in the best way. "I have a few more waiting for you." He settled on Shiloh's lap again, pleased how well he fit there.

"Oh, I like that." Shiloh's hand wrapped around the back of his neck, and slowly drew him in for another of those kisses that felt never-ending. The big chore that he'd been holding back over—getting that smoker set up—wasn't a worry anymore, so he let himself get lost in the moment, enjoying every taste, every time his tongue slid along Shiloh's, every touch of Shiloh's heavy lips.

Shiloh's hands dragged over his back, the touch heated, even through his sweater. He pressed a hand against Shiloh's chest, surprised at the hard resistance and spread his fingers, tracing the muscle there.

Whoa. Who would have known that there was a hardbody under the boring clothes? Tate was interested in seeing the parts he was touching. He tucked a couple of fingers between the buttons in Shiloh's shirt. "We saw the sunset. It's getting dark."

"Mmhmm. We don't want to freeze solid." Shiloh smiled against his lips.

"No, right? We should take our drinks inside. Maybe put a fire on. Get warm."

"Sounds perfect." Shiloh stood, bringing him along.

Tate scooped up his beer and followed, happy to be led, happy to have his hand in Shiloh's bigger one. Just basically happy to have the man here.

They got the fire going, then they settled on the sofa, both of them putting their drinks on the table with harmonizing clicks. He grinned over at Shiloh, then slid a hand over the cowboy's knee. "It's a comfy couch."

Shiloh's thigh tightened, then his legs spread under the touch. The response was heady. "It is."

Okay. Cool. He took that to mean they were on the same page. He wasn't sure what else was on that page, but it seemed like they were ready to find out. "You're good at lighting fires, cowboy. You've had some practice I guess?"

"I have. It's been a while, but I imagine it's a little like riding a horse. A few fumbles, and you're back in the saddle."

Oh, ho! His lips stretched into a wide grin, and he climbed right over so he was straddling Shiloh's knees. "This is a good game. I love all this innuendo."

Shiloh's chuckle went straight to his sac, even as those hands went right on his ass. "I'm sure I got no idea what you're talkin' about..."

Uh-huh. No idea. No clue. He had to swallow before he spoke because his mouth had gone dry. "Really? Well, shit. Maybe I should just stop talking then." He bit his lip and reached for Shiloh's shirt, fingers working open the first few buttons. "I'm more interested in what's under here anyway."

Shiloh's hands tightened, and he felt the moan as much as he heard it. "You ain't gonna hear me complaining."

Oh god, that sound made him ache. He leaned harder

into Shiloh's hands. "Okay. Good." His fingers were trembling a little as he unbuttoned as low as he could, still hardly believing this was happening. Then he tugged on the soft shirt to free it from Shiloh's jeans so he could get to the last couple.

Look at that belly. He didn't know why someone would hide that under layers, but he was damn happy to be the lucky man uncovering it.

"You're a fucking stud under that shirt. Damn." He slid his fingers over skin and soft fuzzy hair, gaze following his fingers and taking it all in.

"Mmm...thank you." Shiloh flexed for him, a soft sigh filling the air. "Damn, that's fine."

The cowboy could just keep talking. That deep voice and low tone sent shivers up his spine. He lifted his gaze to Shiloh's, then reached back and tugged off his sweater, which he dropped somewhere—the floor, the coffee table, he didn't care—then did the same with the T-shirt beneath, baring skin a lot paler than Shiloh's and covered in a lot more goosebumps too.

Shiloh hummed and started touching, mapping his skin and letting him feel strong and sensual. He slid his hands up higher, over Shiloh's shoulders to his neck and pulled him into another kiss. A harder one, letting Shiloh feel everything the man was doing to him.

A harsh groan sounded, and Shiloh was feasting on him, tongue exploring him and fucking his lips. Tate couldn't help his needy moan, he wanted more. He pushed away the thought that he should have more patience; he just couldn't anymore, and dropped his hands to Shiloh's fly.

He found the solid metal buckle, popped it open, and pulled the belt loose. The prize that was hiding under those jeans was more than generous. Holy fuck he wanted a taste of that. He worked Shiloh's heavy cock free and circled his fingers around the thick shaft. "Damn, cowboy."

"Oh, fuck." Shiloh's eyes crossed, tongue flicking out to wet his lips. "Your hands."

He stroked gently. "Soon to be my lips if you want them."

"If?" Shiloh pushed up toward his fingers, cheeks flushed. "Any man in his right mind would want, and I'm not crazy."

He grinned slowly, hotly, and let Shiloh see it. "No, you are not." He slid off Shiloh's lap and tugged on the cowboy's jeans, making more room so he could fondle those hot balls too, then knelt right between Shiloh's knees and blew across the head of the hungry cock.

"Dammit..." Shiloh spread, belly rippling as he arched up, just barely, just enough to barely spread his lips.

When he'd decided he was okay being single forever he'd obviously forgotten how much he liked being wanted. His own cock filled in response, and he groaned as he touched his tongue to Shiloh's slit, taking just a taste of what was to come. Bitter and salty, almost smoky—Shiloh had a flavor all his own, and Tate found himself groaning again as Shiloh did.

He opened up and let the big head through, a little wide-eyed at the stretch in his cheeks, but it was the best mouthful he'd had in a long time. The head of Shiloh's cock hit the roof of his mouth and slid farther back, and he worked on getting just the right angle in case Shiloh was the run-with-it type.

"Oh, Sunshine, that's fine. I can't hold it too terrible long."

Tate took that as a compliment. He pressed a hand into Shiloh's abs and focused on making the cowboy howl.

It didn't take long, but the sharp bark of need satisfied

Tate deep down, and then Shiloh's need splashed on his tongue.

He loved Shiloh's rough breath and sated little grunts and moans as he licked and nuzzled. He shifted his kisses to Shiloh's hard abs and worked his way up, tasting a dark little nipple on the way and nosing into the fuzz at Shiloh's sternum.

"Jesus..." Shiloh grabbed him up, drawing him into a hard kiss that proved that his new lover wasn't all sweet, not by any means. He melted against the cowboy, his startled sound turning needy and muffled by their kiss, and all that heat went straight to his balls.

Shiloh had his jeans undone before he even knew it, and those callused hands worked his cock from base to tip with a sure touch that curled his toes.

"Oh fuck. Oh Jesus. Fuck." That big fist was rough and gentle at once, and he arched into Shiloh's hand without a single rational thought. He wanted, and Shiloh had exactly what he needed.

"Yeah." Shiloh never let up, the touch burning him right to the ground. "So goddamn pretty."

His mouth dropped open and he let his head roll back, barely getting a breath as his heart pounded in his ears. "Shi —oh!" He didn't even think to warn Shiloh when he felt the dam breaking; he just gave into it with a cry, rocking with the waves that followed.

The touch gentled, but it didn't disappear. It just kept the aftershocks going on and on until they were almost unbearable.

"S—stop. Shi. Fuck, you're killing me." He chuckled, pushing on Shiloh's arm, still trying to catch his breath. "Oh, god."

"Mmm...you smell good." Okay, that was hot as hell, those rough words in Shiloh's smooth voice.

"You're a fucking stud." He reached for his T-shirt and used it to wipe down Shiloh's abs, perfectly happy to have an excuse to ogle them again. "How were you hiding all this under loose clothes?"

"This what, Sunshine?"

He chuckled. "You're joking right? All this muscle. The six-pack. When you've got this, you need to show it off."

"Oh, I'm just alone a lot. Not much to do but pull-ups and the food channels."

"Oh, gosh. Not much to do but give myself washboard abs and keep the hottest cock ever to myself." He gave Shiloh a coy grin, teasing.

"You turkey." Shiloh pinched one of his nipples—not hurting but proving that there was a sense of humor in there.

"Ow!" He protested anyway. "So serious. That was fucking hot, man." He shifted back onto the couch so he could tuck back in and found Shiloh's shirt for him. "I'm going to get a clean T-shirt. You need anything?"

"I need to borrow your bathroom, and then I'll put on a sweatshirt so I don't freeze."

"Such a shame to cover up all...that." He sighed dramatically and gestured to Shiloh with an open hand. "You know where the bathroom is. I'll use the one in the bedroom." They'd have to go do whatever Shiloh needed to do with the smoker soon, and it was chilly out, so sadly, shirts were probably a good idea.

Shiloh's soft chuckle followed him, chased him into his bedroom.

"Hey!" He laughed, his walk turning into a quick shuffle. "Your bathroom is out there, big guy."

"Yes, sir. I see how it is." There was that warm laughter again, and Tate could get used to hearing it.

"You do? All right then." He pulled Shiloh into the bathroom and wet a washcloth, drawing it slowly down the cowboy's chest, over his hard abs and around Shiloh's hefty prick. "Is this how it is?"

"Oh, sweet fuck." Shiloh's eyes crossed. "You make me a little stupid."

"Good." He scrubbed Shiloh clean, then dried him off and took his time buttoning up his shirt again. "Now, go get your sweatshirt, cowboy. And then you can show me what to do with the smoker."

"It's crazy easy. You just put the soaked wood chips in the smoker every now and again." Shiloh grinned at him, winked.

"Okay, then. Stay." He tossed that washcloth and grabbed another, taking his time washing up as well.

"Stay? Like right here?"

"Mmm. No. Here." He pulled Shiloh back into the bedroom and opened a drawer in his dresser to find a new shirt. He pulled it on, then pulled Shiloh over to his closet. "Here, now. I need a clean sweater."

"A clean sweater..." One of Shiloh's hands cupped the curve of his ass.

"Mhm." He pulled it on, grinning. This was fun. "Where's your sweatshirt, caveman?"

"Sitting out in your kitchen in my bag."

"Okay." He tucked his fingers into Shiloh's belt and tugged him along. "You're a little high on hormones, huh?"

"A little, yeah. It's been a while." Shiloh flushed, skin going hot against his fingers.

"You're a handsome one." He stopped by Shiloh's bag.

"You really are. I can't believe I let you sit there by yourself all this time."

"Nonsense. I'm just a dude in a bar." Said dude tugged him close though, and gave him a deep, slow kiss.

He was left breathless and blushing, leaning hard on Shiloh. "A...really hot dude in a bar." Damn. Now he couldn't think. How was he going to keep his mind on building tomorrow? And behave himself with all those people around?

"Mmhmm..." One that obviously loved kissing, because Shiloh dove in again.

He was all over that. He had nothing but time for Shiloh, to kiss, or anything else the man had in mind. Literally anything. He whimpered in surrender and put an arm around Shiloh's nape just to help him keep his feet, still holding onto that belt for dear life.

Shiloh was like diving into the ocean. There was no end, no bottom, nothing but sensation and light. The cowboy smelled like mountain air and wood smoke, his tongue was rough and hungry, and every nerve in Tate's body tingled. He knew what he wanted; he'd be happy for Shiloh to have him—bend him over the kitchen counter, fuck him on the couch, take him to bed—anything. But he didn't know what Shiloh was ready for, and he was hell-bent not to push Shiloh too far. He didn't need to rush, but that didn't make him want the cowboy any less.

"Jesus, I could do this for days." Shiloh nibbled on his bottom lip, tugging, but so gentle.

He chuckled weakly. "Sooner...sooner or later... everyone's got to breathe." He wasn't much at the moment, just hanging on tight.

"And put more wood in the smoker and have our drinks and..." And their lips came together again.

"And...yeah. Whatever you...anything you want." Tate shifted and went up on his toes, fingers curling into Shiloh's shirt. "Anything you want."

"I want—I want you." Shiloh met his eyes. "But no pressure. Seriously."

"Fuck yes. Where? How?" He didn't care one bit if he seemed eager.

"Bed? Is that... I don't want to intrude on you, but..."

The bed was fine. Awkward, but fine. "No, bed's good. I —" He grinned sheepishly. "I just need to make it. Like, put clean sheets on it and stuff."

"I'll help. I totally know how to do that."

Okay, cool. Shiloh didn't make that weird. He headed for the bedroom again. "Thanks. I—it's a brand-new bed. I've never slept in it. I bought the house, put the bed in and... I sleep on the couch." He shrugged and opened his closet. "I bought sheets, they're washed and everything, but who knows how long they've been on. I need to change them."

"I'll grab this side." Shiloh was telling the truth. He totally knew how to make a bed, smooth out the sheets, everything. The bed looked pretty good all made up. He pulled out a soft blanket which he bought for the bed but usually used on the couch. He'd put it away for company.

"We don't want to freeze our—uh...butts off."

"No. No freezing off parts." Shiloh chuckled and squeezed his hand. "I like parts."

"This is going to be the first time I've slept—or not slept I guess—in this bed. Don't you feel special?" He felt like a weirdo, but Shiloh hadn't made him feel that way, it was just a thing.

"Yeah. Let me put some chips in the smoker, and I'll be right back for you." Shiloh grinned, the look a little sheepish. "I don't think I'm going to be able to stop in the middle, right?"

He laughed. "If you did, I might not let you come back after."

Shiloh grinned at him and then ran out, and he heard the kitchen door open, smelled the wood smoke.

11

What was he doing?

What on earth was he thinking?

Shiloh filled the wood box and tried not to panic. He couldn't believe he'd just basically asked Tate if they could have sex.

He had never been the forward one. Not once.

It had felt pretty damn good. He might do it again.

Making the bed was some new kind of foreplay he knew nothing about, but Tate clearly hadn't made assumptions, and that was probably a good thing. Respectful. Maybe short-sighted, but respectful.

He peeked in on the meat, which was doing what it was supposed to do, and figured he should wander back into the house. Tate was waiting on him.

He headed back inside, locking up the house and making a beeline for the bedroom. With his luck, Tate had fallen asleep.

But he had much better luck today. There was music playing in the bedroom, and he could see from the hall that just one little bedside lamp was on. When he entered the room, he found that Tate had stripped down to nothing and was drinking water with his back to the door, perfect pale ass right there for him to admire.

"Oh, you are pretty as all get out." He stepped out of his boots and stripped off his sweatshirt.

Tate set his water down and turned around, cheeks rosy, hopefully from his compliment. "I've been told I'm skinny."

"I've been told I'm unfriendly." He pushed down his jeans.

"I beg to differ; you've been very friendly to me." Tate stepped closer and kissed his bare shoulder. "So friendly."

"And you're very fine to me, so we're even steven." His nipples went hard, and he drew Tate toward the bed.

"Even steven? People still say that?" Tate winked and scooted away quickly, climbing up on the bed.

He swatted that pretty butt playfully as he followed like a dog on a leash. Right. That was why he'd asked to have sex.

Tate propped up on his side. "Hey there, handsome." A hot hand slid over his abs and circled the base of his cock. "Wanna fuck?"

"You know it, Sunshine." He'd been with the toughest sons of bitches on earth. He was going to do his best to drive Tate out of his mind. He tugged Tate into a kiss designed to burn them both to the ground.

Tate moaned into it, fingers sliding down his length, working the tip against his palm. His prick filled like a balloon, just hard and aching in a couple three strokes.

He groaned and cupped Tate's ass, fingers curling in to tease the crease.

"Yeah," Tate whispered against his lips. "I want that. I want you." Tate abandoned his prick, hands moving over his chest and shoulders instead. "Fuck, Shiloh."

He nodded, his muscles clenching. God, this was like a wet dream, but it was all too real. He pulled their hips together, making Tate moan again and arch against him. Tate hooked a leg around his thigh keeping them close together.

"You feel so good." Tate kissed him again, lips crashing against his and—

And a phone was ringing.

He frowned as Tate went still, pulling back. "You need to get that?"

Tate sighed. "I...well, it's really weird for me to get a call at his hour." The phone stopped ringing but rang again a breath later. "Yeah. I better get it. It's in the kitchen."

"Okay..." He backed off, letting Tate get up off the bed.

"Sorry. I'm sorry..." Tate scurried toward the kitchen, naked ass disappearing through the bedroom door. "Hello? Hey, Paul, everything okay?" Tate wandered back into the room with the phone. "Oh man. Is he okay? Oh, yeah. Definitely. Send me a pin. It's no trouble, really."

Okay, that sounded like, "Put your clothes on, Shiloh" to him. He got out of the bed and grabbed his sweats.

"I'll have him text you when I get there. Sure. You're welcome. See you soon." Tate tossed the phone on the bed and started pulling on clothing. "My friend's son swerved to avoid a deer and ended up in some kind of ditch. He lives farther up the mountain."

"Oh no! Can I help, or should I just hold down the house?" Lord have mercy, that sounded scary as all get out.

"Well...the smoker?" Tate pulled on socks. "Can we leave it?"

"I don't see why not. Let me get my jeans and all." He wasn't going anywhere in boots and sweats. Then his phone began to ring. "What the hell?"

Sky's ringtone. Figured.

"Rains it pours? Where is your phone?"

"Uh..." On the sofa? Probably the sofa. They'd been less than careful there.

"Hang on. I'll follow the ring. My shoes are out there anyway." Tate left the bedroom and quickly shouted, "Got it! You want me to answer it?"

"Sure, go ahead. It's Sky. You met him at the bar." This should be interesting.

"Hey, Sky. This is Tate, we met at a bar in town? Hang on Shiloh's right here...one sec." Tate brought the phone to him and handed it off before hurrying to the bathroom. "I'm just gonna pee real quick."

"Okay. Sure."

"I—hey. Just, uh. Damn, Sam. What are you up to?"

"Nothing. Nothing. Someone Tate knows needs help is all." God, he felt sweaty, acidy, and a little shaky.

"You're...wait, you're at Tate's now? Tonight?" Sky sounded more than a little curious.

"Yes. Yes, I'm smoking briskets and a ham." *And I was going to get it on, dammit.*

"Oh, right. That's an...all-night event." Sky was implying exactly what he wasn't getting.

"It is." And his cheeks were on fire. On fucking fire. "You'll thank me tomorrow."

Sky chuckled. "Well, I am looking forward to this. I'm sure you'll be having a very good day."

"I hope so. I'm looking forward to making new friends. See you tomorrow?" He was dressed now—boots to jacket and hat.

"Yeah. Still okay to bring the kids for a bit? Charlie is chomping at the bit to see you."

"Yeah, as far as I know. Tate? It's still cool for Sky and Beck to bring the kids for a little while?"

"You know it. You ready?" Tate walked right by him and left the bedroom. "Where are my keys? Crap."

"I am. What do they look like?" Shiloh started glancing around, still on the phone. "Tate says yes."

"They're on a Red Sox key ring."

"Great. Go be a hero, cowboy. We'll see you tomorrow. Hang up."

"Wait. I got 'em." Tate grabbed a coat, stomped into a pair of work boots and opened the front door. "Don't worry about the lights. Fuck, it's cold out here."

"Yessir. It's plumb bitter." He'd have thought Tate would be used to it. He was still pretty new at this whole deep winter thing.

Tate locked up the house, then hurried to his truck and started it up. "We'll have heat in a minute." Tate's hand landed on his thigh. "I'm sorry about this. I...wanted something else. Obviously."

"No worries, Sunshine. You're being a good man. That's important." And maybe he needed to take a step back, a breath.

"If it were my kid...you know? I'd want someone to show up." Tate took off down the dark, rural road at a good clip. He seemed fidgety and impatient. "He's just a couple of minutes up the mountain."

"I do know." And he respected the hell out of it, too. "You're a good egg."

"A good egg that just ruined our evening together." Tate snorted. "I'll make it up to you." Tate slowed and took a left turn, literally heading *up* the mountain. The road was narrow and unpaved, mostly packed gravel and dirt. "See the drainage ditch on that side? It's deep because the water runoff up here when the snow melts is no joke. It's not hard to dip into it, and it's not easy to get out of."

"Oh, I bet. I upended into a ditch when I was learning how to drive. I was so damn embarrassed." He'd been distracted by a boy, of course.

Tate snorted. "I've never done that, but it's never too late. There he is." Tate pulled up near the kid's truck and they climbed out.

"Mr. Dutton?" God, the poor kid looked wide-eyed and worried.

"Hey, Jimmy. Your dad sent me, it's a hike from the valley. You okay?"

"Yeah. No? I don't know."

"Does anything hurt? Tingle?" Shiloh held out one hand. "Shiloh. Pleased."

"Jimmy. Embarrassed."

Shiloh chuckled. "Yeah. We all have our moments, man."

"I'm a little stiff but everything moves." Jimmy shrugged. "Except the truck."

Shiloh nodded. "No, that looks pretty stuck."

"Dad's gonna kill me." Jimmy shook his head.

"I don't think so. He sent me, right? He's just glad you're okay."

"Accidents happen, man. What happened?" Shiloh would bet someone was texting.

"A deer jumped out; there's a run back there. I swerved, and the one wheel started to go, and I just couldn't stop it."

"You have to watch your speed up here," Tate suggested carefully.

Jimmy nodded. "Mhm."

"Evil friggin' deer." No reason to make the kid feel worse, right?

Lights came at them from down the road. "That's either your dad or the tow truck."

Jimmy nodded, looking nervous. It turned out to be the tow truck, and the guy pulled up, lights flashing. "Everyone okay?"

"I am. The car..."

"Yeah, your dad said. Sucks, but we'll get it out." The tow truck guy started doing his thing, and Shiloh thought it was like having a truck of cowboys pull up. Just stay out of their way and let them do their job.

"That guy knows what he's doing, huh?" Tate slipped a hand into his. "We'll be off the hook soon."

"It's cool. Should we bring Jimmy back down to the house?" They surely weren't going to leave the kid to wait.

"Oh. Yeah, maybe we should. I can get him a Coke, and you can check on your smoker. I'll go ask him." Tate squeezed his hand and kissed his cheek before heading over to Jimmy, who was watching the whole operation nervously.

Poor kid—nothing like being reminded your teacher is human.

The ride back to the house was quiet, partly because Jimmy was texting the whole way. Maybe his dad, his friends, who knew? But the plan was to hang out at the house until Jimmy's dad showed up. It wouldn't be long.

Tate pulled into the driveway, and they piled out. "You want a Coke, or I can make some coffee? You think your dad would want coffee?"

"Pop would take coffee. I'd love a Coke, please. I have a headache."

"You oughta check his eyes, hmm?" Shiloh whispered under his breath. "Make sure the pupils are the same size?"

Tate nodded once, acknowledging him. "Sure. Come on in the bathroom, let me get you some Tylenol. Do you remember if you hit your head? Maybe on the steering wheel or the door? Shi, can you put some coffee on?"

"Absolutely." He could do that, no problem, and check the smoker. Coffee. Water. He did love these old-school carafes.

"I don't know. Maybe? I don't know." Jimmy followed Tate, and when they came back, Tate went right to the freezer for an ice pack.

"He's got a bump, left side. Good call."

He was about to respond when the doorbell rang.

"I got it. Jimmy, put this on your head. Here's your Coke."

"Th—thank you."

"Have a sit, man. I seen a lot of those. You'll be okay. Maybe have your folks worried about you for a couple days, that's all."

Jimmy shrugged at him. "Okay."

Tate and Jimmy's dad talked out on the porch for a minute, and were both nice and calm when they came back in.

"Shiloh, this is Paul. Paul, Shiloh."

"Hey, Shiloh." Paul shook his hand as he stood. "Thanks for your help with this."

"No worries. There's coffee brewing, if you'd like a cup."

"That would be great. Thank you." Paul went to Jimmy and sat down. The poor kid looked like he was ready to fly to pieces. "Hey, Jim. You okay?"

"I'm sorry, Dad."

"It's okay. Accidents happen. So, Tate—Mr. Dutton—said you have a headache?"

"I hit my head I guess? I don't remember. It hurts a little now that I know about it. I'm okay though. I am. I'm good."

"Yeah. I bet you are. Still, let's not do that again, deal?"

Shiloh poured three mugs of coffee, but he didn't know

how they took them, so he brought them and a gallon of milk to the table.

Jimmy snorted. "Yeah. No."

"Mhm." Paul picked up his coffee and sipped it black. "I got a call about the Jeep. It's not too bad. The mechanic will get back to me tomorrow. So you avoided a deer?"

"Yeah. I turned the wheel a little hard I guess." Jimmy shrugged and sipped his Coke.

"It happens. Your mother bounced up and down a tunnel for something just like that."

"She bounced...? What?" Jimmy looked up from his Coke for the first time since it was handed to him.

"Seriously. She was in a Mustang convertible and a bird flew into the car and she panicked and totaled that hot little car."

Jimmy's eyes went wide. "Oh my god. That's scary."

"She didn't drive again for over a year. It terrified her."

There was a saying about falling off a horse that fit here, but it wasn't Shiloh's place to say it.

Jimmy put his Coke down. "I have to wait a year?"

"No, I wasn't saying that I just—never mind. We should probably get going, because it's late." Paul turned to Tate. "I really appreciate you running up there. We didn't want him alone."

"I totally get it. Especially if he'd been hurt or something. You might want to watch that head."

"Yeah. We will. If it's not better in the morning, his mom will probably want to take him to see someone." Paul stood and took a big swig, swallowing down the last of his coffee. "That hit the spot. Thanks again, Shiloh."

"Of course. Nice to meet you." He held out his hand to shake, and Paul took it.

"Ditto. I'll see you around, huh?"

Shiloh nodded. He hoped so, yeah.

Jimmy hauled himself up off the couch, and Tate reached out to steady him. "You good?"

"Yeah. Yeah, it's not my head, I'm just...shaky."

"Adrenaline probably. Come on, kid, let's get you home."

Tate saw them out, walking them to their car and making sure Jimmy got in okay, then he jogged back to the house, hands in his pockets. "Chilly."

"It is. I need to check that smoker here in a minute. You think he's okay?" Were he and Tate okay?

"Yeah. I think so. He's in good hands in any case. Paul's a good guy." Tate started cleaning up glasses and mugs.

"You work together, you said?" God, this was awkward.

"Yeah, he teaches history. He's like the AP guru. AP US History." Tate set the mugs in the sink, then stepped in close to him. "I am so sorry."

"Don't be. You were that kid's hero, and a good friend." He let himself wrap his arms around Tate and hold on.

Tate burrowed in, nuzzling his chest. "Not the best date though."

"I don't know." He stroked Tate's back. "We both had orgasms. That's pretty impressive."

Tate sighed. "That did not suck." They stood there for a bit, just being close. "Should we stoke that smoker?"

"We so should." He kissed Tate's shoulder. "I'll be back in two shakes."

Or maybe a few more, just to clear his head. He thought he needed it.

12

"Did you see Beck lift that lumber up onto his shoulder? How hot was that?"

Tate glanced over at Skyler and Beckett who were drinking well-earned beers. They'd worked their asses off, as had everyone who had come by to help Shiloh get his greenhouse up. Shiloh was still going to have to build whatever he needed for the inside, but they'd cleared the ground and put up the main structure, which they'd never have been able to do alone.

Beckett was handsome enough. But Shiloh was the hot one. He was leaning against the side of the house while they talked, drinking water with one eye on the smoker. It smelled amazing. He didn't think Shiloh had gotten any sleep with all the fussing over it he'd done all night, but that didn't stop him from working harder than anyone today.

Shiloh was the most focused person he'd ever known, seriously. Serious and sure, absolutely focused on whatever he was doing. It was heady, when you got right down to it.

"You made him blush." Shiloh grinned, teasing.

Beckett snorted. "I do not blush. I like building though. It looks great, Shiloh."

"I hope we can get some amazing food growing—I'm planning kale, spinach, brussels sprouts, and broccoli to start." Shiloh beamed at him. "I really appreciate this."

"Sounds great." Sky looked the greenhouse over, smiling. "Matt would love this. To see you getting your hands back into the earth. He always said you could make anything grow."

Shiloh nodded, and a small shadow passed over his expression, then disappeared. "I do love digging in the dirt."

Tate wanted to take his hand, but he just didn't know. So awkward not knowing. "It's going to be nice to have more company out here, and have the land used to grow things like it should be. If it works out, and you like it, in the spring we can clear even more land."

Shiloh grinned at him, and the look was...maybe a little intense, a little hot.

Sky turned to Beckett. "I get the feeling we're missing some important details here."

"Don't you? Always the last to know..." Beckett turned his grin on Shiloh.

"Shut up, lawyer man." Shiloh rolled his eyes. "You're a shit."

He did take Shiloh's hand then; he knew whose side he was on in this game. "It's just a new thing. We're going slow."

"Hey, no one's judging. Teasing, sure, but judging?" Sky nodded and winked. "Never."

"Shiloh's been off the market a while, is all, and it's nice to see a spark, you know?"

"We're a little past a spark, I think." He wanted another one of those looks. The heated ones.

"Just a...touch." Okay, that was surprisingly hot, that low, soft voice, meant just for him. It made his skin tingle and his mouth dry.

"So do we get to taste this brisket, or was that a lie just to get us to help?" Beckett leaned back in his chair and sipped his beer.

They all knew it was the real thing; it smelled amazing, and there was no escaping it. Even his crew from the bar—the ones who'd showed up—were starting to glance toward the smoker. "I'll get the sides set up." They'd dug up every platter he owned to put the food on and a stack of paper plates.

"There are two briskets and a ham. You want to carve, Sky?" Shiloh headed for the smoker, motioning his friend over.

"You know it." Sky followed, and Beckett jumped out of his chair.

"I'll help carry."

"Great. Thanks." Inside he started pulling the side dishes he'd bought out of the fridge. Potato salad, pasta salad and coleslaw. "Not fancy, but edible."

"Listen, one thing I've learned hanging out with Texans? They eat better at a barbeque than we do."

"I bet. Shiloh is a great cook."

"Sky too. It's a thing. Enjoy it and hit the gym." Beck chuckled. "It's nice to see him outside of that bar."

Tate nodded. "I think we might have something." He had to be careful though. Part of him wanted to move fast, and part of him was worried he'd send Shiloh running.

"He's been lonely. Sky was worried he'd just fade into nothing."

"He was trying hard, that's for sure." He picked up a couple of dishes and Beckett got a couple as well.

"Well, I wish you both luck. The kids were over the moon to get invited over to see your 'milky cows'."

"They're welcome any time." He kicked the door open and held it for Beckett with his foot. "Long table over there."

"Over by the expert carver." Shiloh was arranging meat onto platters while Skyler carved away. "Hey, stud." Beckett kissed Sky's neck, then set the food down. "This is going to be quite a spread."

"Mmm... I taste-tested. Oh my god, we're so hiring him for the event. I swear." Sky grinned up at Beck.

"Hiring Shiloh? Cool." Tate put the food down, his fingers ghosting over Shiloh's ass as he moved away.

Shiloh jumped, but the glance he got suited him to the bone. Tate winked back. Maybe they'd get a second chance tonight.

"Hey, everyone," Tate shouted, waving to his friends who were scattered all over the backyard. "Come on and eat!"

There was plenty, and the sounds of happy eating and praise for Shiloh's food made Tate beam. Shiloh was modest, but the expression on the cowboy's face was utterly pleased.

"Uncle Shiloh!" A little boy came around the side of the house, running full out and headed for Shiloh, with a toddler right on his heels.

"Uh-oh." Tate grinned and reached over to take Shiloh's plate. "I got this." He got out of the way quickly.

"My favorite kiddos!" Shiloh knelt down and opened his arms. "I've missed your kisses!"

They attacked as only kids could, tangling themselves in Shiloh's arms. While they were busy getting hugs and smooches, a taller girl with a woman Tate also hadn't seen before rounded the house, but they went right to Skyler and Beckett. So these were their kids. Wow.

The older girl leaned up against the side of the house with her arms crossed, watching Shiloh carefully. He knew that look. That was the you're on my shit list look. And she did it well. He was absolutely not going to grin, however.

Shiloh let the other two go, and then went to kneel down across from the little girl. "I suck. I'm sorry. I was very busy being sad, and I messed up. I forgot that you'd miss me as much as I missed you. I was wrong."

She seemed to think about that carefully, looking right into Shiloh's eyes, then gave him a gentle hug. "I'm sorry you're sad. I was sad once too."

"I know. You lost your folks. I lost my husband. But I am so sorry I hurt your feelings. That was mean of me." Shiloh kissed her hand. "Can we be friends again?"

She grinned and cut her eyes toward the smoker. "Is that brisket?"

"You know it. You hungry, cowgirl?"

"Starving!" She ran over to the table and grabbed a plate. "Brisket me, Uncle Shiloh!"

"Brisket!" The other two found plates and lined up.

He wandered over to Beckett. "So these are yours?"

"The whole bunch. The big one is Charlie, then Noah and Sierra. This is Lacey, she looks after them when we're... well, at a barbeque and greenhouse raising."

"Hey, Lacey. Go grab some food, there's a ton of it."

"Sounds great. Thank you."

"Is Charlie limping?" He watched her moving, it sure looked like she was.

"She came off a horse yesterday." Skyler nodded, not seeming the least bit concerned.

"Rodeo." Beckett rolled his eyes. "Barrel racing practice. She takes after this guy."

"Oh, wow. She...is she okay?"

"She's fine. She'll remember to keep her heels down next time." Sky didn't seem worried at all.

He loved watching Shiloh with the kids, and he could tell that they just adored him. They climbed over the cowboy and stole bites and jabbered and laughed and asked questions, and Shiloh was there for it.

Lacey got some food and a beer and wandered into the crowd of his friends like she knew them. The handful of guys were happy to have her there, and why not? She was pretty. Tate chuckled and wandered over to Shiloh and the kids. "Got your hands full, huh?"

"Never." Shiloh tickled the little boy, making him giggle. "Did you get yourself a plate?"

Right, food. And it all looks so good. "Oh, I better do that. I was waiting for everyone else? You?" He picked up a plate and started helping himself to brisket.

"I've been picking as I cooked, but yeah, I totally need to." Shiloh grinned and grabbed a plate of his own.

"Kids," Skyler called out. "Go run around and play and let Shiloh eat."

"Yes, sir." The little ones took off running, and Charlie went to sit with her dads.

"They seem like nice kids."

"They're glorious. Charlie and Noah are adopted, and then little Sierra was with a surrogate. They're amazing together." Shiloh tilted his head. "I never thought of Skyler as a dad, back when he was riding with Matty, but he's amazing."

"Well, all you really need is to want to." He shrugged. "And I guess a little creativity. From what I understand, from there you make everything up as you go along. Do you want to be a dad someday?" Oh. Crap. That was—he'd meant that as small talk, but it sounded like a loaded question.

"You—uh. You don't have to answer that if you don't want to."

"I don't know. My life is different now, in every way. I'm trying to figure a lot of sh-shtuff out." Shiloh chuckled, and the sound was wry. "I guess I'm learning, teach."

"There's a lot of *shtuff* to learn." He laughed. Objectively, he thought Shiloh would make a great dad. He was gentle and thoughtful, he understood family. Tate wanted kids—like a dozen of them. Or four. He'd settle on four. But he didn't believe for a second that was in his future; that would be setting himself up for disappointment.

"Yeah." Shiloh blinked a little, and then this warm smile bloomed, meaning something he wasn't sure he understood. "A ton."

"You're a mysterious man, you know. Starting with this brisket. Oh my god." He took another bite, chewing and grinning like he'd never had real food before.

"It's good, isn't it? I haven't lost my touch." Shiloh ate a bite himself, and Tate was fascinated by this new, relaxed Shiloh. It was like Shiloh had a dozen faces.

"You want to stay the night again?" It was Saturday, and he wanted a second chance.

Shiloh's grin deepened, cheeks going rosy. "I was hoping you'd ask."

"Yeah? Good." He felt himself blush too, heat setting his ears on fire. "Good."

"Yeah." Shiloh chuckled as people started showing up for round two. "Time to carve the brisket."

He got out of Shiloh's way but stayed close enough to watch and admire. This made Shiloh happy. It was in every slice of smoked meat.

He thought he knew how to make the cowboy even happier though.

13

E veryone was gone.
There was a greenhouse. There were leftovers for tomorrow. The world smelled like sawdust and smoke, and Shiloh was sitting on the sofa with Tate, drinking his whiskey.

It was a thousand times better than being in the bar.

They even had their feet up on the coffee table. In socks. Tate was tucked into the crook of his arm and was sipping some kind of hot tea with a little brandy in it, there was a fire going, and it felt just like he belonged here.

"What an incredible day."

"It was. It was amazing. Thank you." He dared to brush a kiss over Tate's temple. It was the best day he'd had since Matty had gone. That hurt a little, but it wasn't awful, just sad.

And he didn't feel like he was being tugged down into a well. He was physically tired, and there was a reason—there was a greenhouse, there had been a party. Hell, there had been orgasms.

"You know who else looked happy? Your friends Sky and

Beckett. I think they're happy for you. They were super helpful too."

"Sky is a good guy, and the more I know Beck, the more I like him." Beck and Sky had been separated a lot of the time when he'd known them with Matty. Hell, Matty was gone by the time the babies had come. "And those kids give me extreme joy."

Charlie had broken his heart, but just because he was down didn't mean he got to hurt a little girl that loved him. She'd lost so much, and he was going to keep that in mind.

Matty was dead, but there were people who loved him who were alive.

Tate at least liked him, and was warm and snuggling on the couch, fingers sliding up under Shiloh's shirt.

"Mmm...your hands feel good." He sighed and leaned into the touch.

"The day isn't over yet. You ready to turn in?"

"I am." They had a little unfinished business, he thought. "Thank you for today. Have I said?"

"Maybe. But I didn't do more than anyone else. And you did all the cooking." Tate stood, holding a hand out for him to come along.

He took that hand, tingles sliding up his arm. If he did this—went to bed with Tate like this, he was admitting that he wanted to live again.

I'm sorry, Matty.

He stood, squeezing Tate's fingers.

Tate squeezed back, silently, as if answering a question. He followed where he was led, and Tate was turning off lights and locking doors as they went, putting the house to bed too. The bedroom was dark, but Tate turned one small light on.

"You know what I want," Tate said softly. "But please

don't let me rush you. We have all the time we need—days, weeks ahead of us. I teach high school; that's the definition of patience."

He cupped Tate's jaw and kissed him. "That's the nicest thing anyone's ever said to me."

"I teach high school?" Tate grinned against his lips.

"Yep. That's it." He nipped Tate's bottom lip.

Tate chuckled and tugged on his shirt. "Show me those abs."

He stripped it off, flexing playfully, waggling his eyebrows to hide his little rush of embarrassment.

"That's what I'm talking about." Tate smoothed his fingers over Shiloh's belly. "Mhm. Don't hide your light, babe. For real."

He'd been afraid his light had gone out altogether, but maybe not. He let himself moan, let Tate feel how good it felt.

"What's your favorite? Face to face? Or do you want my little butt in the air for you? Hm?" Tate was working on his belt, opening his fly.

"I like it all, but this is our first time. I want to see your face." That way he'd know he wasn't doing it wrong.

Tate wiggled his denim down, then tugged off his own shirt. "You're worth the wait, but I'm not answering my phone again tonight."

"Fair enough. I turned mine off." Not that anyone was going to call, but he wasn't taking chances.

Tate climbed up on the bed and settled back on his elbows, naked and showing off, then crooked a finger at him. "I'm ready for you. Get those jeans off and come kiss me."

"Damn, you're pretty." He managed to get his jeans off without falling down or ripping his dick off, which felt like a huge accomplishment. "You got lube and condoms close?"

Had they discussed that last night?

"Yes, I bought them for Friday night out of an abundance of hope." Tate grinned. "Drawer there."

"Excellent. I like a prepared lover." He crawled onto the bed, kissing Tate's ankle, and working his way up. Tate smelled good—smoke and heat and soap and sweat.

"Should we have showered? Do I smell like your brisket? I'd like to be that delicious." Tate was squirming, and goosebumps came up everywhere he kissed.

"Gonna lap you up." He wasn't going to waste this—he wanted to lick and kiss and rev them both up.

"Okay. I'm in. Yes, please." Tate lifted one foot and hooked it over his hip, leaning up for a kiss. He took it, then he offered more kisses—to Tate's nipple, his collarbone, under his ear.

Tate's sigh was heavy with need, and he arched into the attention, responding to everything Shiloh did like his lips were a magnet.

"So friggin' hot." He brought their lips together, cupping Tate's sweet ass and squeezing. He was going to need to get the lube, but it was tough to break away long enough to grab it.

"You just...don't stop." Tate rocked into his hand, ass going tight.

"Not stopping. Promise." He wanted everything; he wanted to touch Tate deep. "Lube. Please."

"Drawer..." Tate stretched an arm out long, fingers groping for the nightstand. He took advantage of the reach to latch on to one nipple, giving it a little attention with lips and tongue.

"Fuck, fuck that's so good." Tate shook his head. "Shi— baby. I can't reach the—oh, fuck."

"Mmhmm..." Okay, this was more fun than color TV. He sucked harder, adding a little teeth to the mix.

"Nono... I mean yes, but...fuck." Tate hadn't stopped moving under him. The hand that had stretched toward the nightstand had given up though, fingers curling into a fist in the sheets.

Oh yes. He switched nipples, giving this one the same treatment.

Another arch, and Tate's heels dug into the mattress. Then, Tate's hand suddenly dove between them and squeezed Shiloh's prick, thumb diving through his slit hard and deep.

He grunted, one hand moving to cup Tate's balls, roll them and add to the pleasure.

"Jesus, Shi—" Tate moaned and shivered, and those sneaky fingers lost their rhythm.

He tapped the skin behind Tate's balls, a wild moan filling his throat as Tate shook and twisted for him. Fuck, he'd never seen anything so pretty.

"Shiloh—please. I need... I...please." Tate's skin was flushed pink from head to toe, and his eyes were unfocused.

He pressed against Tate's tiny little hole, promising what was to come, and he scraped his teeth against Tate's nipple. Tate flailed for the nightstand again but still couldn't reach, and the sound of heated frustration made him grin.

"Come on, babe. I need to take you, feel you come around my cock." Thank god it wasn't all lit up in here, because his cheeks were burning.

Tate grunted, shifting just enough to finally get the drawer open. "You could help, you know!"

"I could, but this is so much fun." He lapped at that swollen little nip.

Tate shoved at him like he was trying to roll them, but he was a taller, stronger, immovable object. "God dammit." Tate's arm somehow grew a foot longer and the drawer slammed open. "In there, you monster." Tate was panting, pulling on him, one big ball of horny impatience.

He reached over and grabbed the lube, wetting his fingers. "Grab a condom for me?"

He pressed the tip of one finger in Tate's tight little hole.

"Asshole." Tate whined and wiggled, and of course got distracted before he finally got his fingers on a condom. "Fuck you. Fuck me."

"I'm going to. Hard. Rubber, Tate." He pushed in deeper, until his finger was all the way in.

"He-here. Oh fuck, yes." Tate bore down on his fingers, clamping around them as he fumbled with the wrapper. He got it open and found his prick with both hands, and burning hot fingers rolled it on all the way to the root.

"Fuck yes." Shiloh slicked himself up, panting hard as he forced himself not to shoot. "You ready or you need more stretching?"

"Good. Ready. Come on, Shi—I want you so fucking bad." Tate hooked both heels around him and lifted right up to meet his cock, taking before he could give it.

"Got you." He eased in, gasping at the tight pressure.

"Oh thank fuck yes. Yes!" Tate relaxed a little, mouth dropping open as his expression grew blissful.

He got it. All the way. He rocked out and pressed in, nice and easy.

Tate matched him, rolling up to meet him and relaxing down again, working in an opposite rhythm. Tate wasn't rushing him now; he was savoring, feeling, losing himself to it all.

Shiloh moaned, letting himself go with the sensation, spin with the way Tate gripped and released him, again and again.

"Oh my god, you're...fuck that's good, Shi." Tate hands settled on his hips, fingers pressing into his skin.

"Better than. Hot as fire." He hoped he was making sense, because his voice was barely more than a growl.

Tate nodded, eyes locking onto his, one dark lock of hair stuck to a damp forehead. "More, baby. Harder. You promised hard."

Oh, fuck yes. He nodded and let himself give Tate everything he wanted to.

"Yes, yes, yes." Tate hung on for the ride, groans and grunts escaping him. Those hands moved from his hips to his ass and tugged him deeper, making Tate's eyes go wide. "Good. So good."

He didn't have the words to answer. All he could do was give Tate all the need he had, his body making promises he fully intended to keep.

They moved together, the room full of their sounds as they rocked and slid like one moving beast until Tate shivered under him and his hands started groping. "Shiloh. Touch me. Please?" Tate was breathless and his voice was rough. "You gotta... I'm so close I just...please?"

"Anything." He was all about getting Tate off before his balls exploded. He reached down and grabbed Tate with a hand that was probably a hint rough. He couldn't help it; he was wild.

Tate rocked into his hand, and it didn't take more than that. Tate howled and shot, ass going tight around him and hot spunk flooding his fingers.

He held on by the skin of his teeth, and as soon as Tate's body relaxed, he began to slam in, burying himself deep inside. His heart beat so hard he felt like it was going to explode.

"Come on, baby." Tate managed between gulps of air, fingers digging into his ass. "Give it up. Show me."

"Yes!" His head snapped back, and he shot, his hips pumping like a piston. For a second, all he could do was feel.

When he could focus again, Tate was a puddle under him, breathing hard and looking totally wrung out, with a soft, goofy smile on his face.

"Wow." That was the most coherent he was going to get.

Tate leaned up and took a quick kiss before collapsing back on the pillows. "You're amazing."

"I feel...whoa." He pulled out, feeling about boneless. It took all he had to stumble to the bathroom to deal with the condom and grab a towel to clean them up before crawling back into bed.

"Mhm. We can sleep late. Nash does Sundays." Tate sounded half asleep already.

"Oh, hell yeah." He sighed and snuggled in. That had sure sounded like an invitation to stay, so he was going to take it.

If he had any doubt, Tate tucked himself close and lay his head on Shiloh's shoulder and he couldn't go anywhere even if he wanted to. "Hell, yeah. Goodnight, Shi. Thanks for a perfect day."

"Thank you." He kissed the top of Tate's head. "For everything."

14

Tate hadn't seen much of Shiloh since last weekend. It was understandable that the guy didn't stay over during the week; Tate had school early and there was no reason for Shiloh to be up and running at just past dawn like he was. He hadn't seen Shiloh at the bar in the evenings either, though, and that was disappointing.

He'd spent far too much time checking out the door, hoping the cowboy would walk in.

He told himself there was a good reason, that Shiloh was probably tired from working every day on the greenhouse, and their schedules just weren't matching up right now. But Shiloh had been at his house, on his land, when he was at school.

It felt weird.

But it was Friday night now, nobody had to get up early-early tomorrow, and he was wishing he were buying two drinks at the bar instead of one.

Maybe...maybe he should just text? Maybe invite Shiloh to supper. Maybe for a booty call.

He'd peeked in the greenhouse, and the work was

astounding. There was this little passive solar heating system, rows of little seedlings in boxes, in pots, even in jars. It was fascinating.

He could call. But what if he was sleeping? What if he'd already had dinner? What if he had other plans?

Okay, he probably didn't have other plans; the man sat in that corner over there every night for while.

He should call. Or text. Less pressure.

He sipped his beer, then pulled out his phone and texted.

He sipped his beer, then pulled out his phone and texted.

> Hey. Hi. You busy?

It took a second, then he got:

> I'm not. You? Also hi.

> I'm drinking alone. You want to join me?

He sent that, and then he thought better of it.

> Or maybe you're hungry?

Or maybe you miss me?

> You at the bar? I can be there in ten. And yes, starving. I'm craving meat.

> At the bar. CU soon.

They were in town; they could wander, go get steaks. He caught himself grinning and took another sip of his beer so he didn't look like an idiot. He was excited to see Shiloh, and he hadn't realized how nervous he'd been about texting. That was silly, obviously, because Shiloh didn't hesitate to meet him.

The cowboy took about ten minutes, but when he walked in the door, Shiloh stole Tate's breath. Black cowboy hat, jeans, and a bright blue button-down—the man was fine.

He slid off his barstool and took a couple of steps in Shiloh's direction, kind of hoping for a kiss hello. He didn't know if he should back off or ask or just go for it. "Hey, you."

"Hey, honey. I missed your face." Shiloh took a brief, warm kiss.

He smiled and pulled Shiloh to the bar. "Yeah? I missed yours too. You've been busy in the greenhouse."

"I've been going to the apartment and crashing. It's good, this physical work, but damn." Shiloh winked at him, put his hat down, brim up.

So it was just what he thought. "Whiskey? Or do you want to go find some food first?" He pulled out his wallet to pay for his beer.

"Let's have some food, and I'll buy you a drink after?" Shiloh stared at him like he was something special.

"Works for me." He put some cash on the bar and took Shiloh's hand. "You are so handsome tonight."

Shiloh's grin was utterly pleased. "Why thank you, sir."

He took Shiloh's arm as they left. "We can walk. Should we get burgers? Or maybe a steak?"

"Oh, I could have a nice steak, I tell you what." Shiloh patted his hand. "How's your week been?"

"Long." *Lonely.* "The kids get itchy when it gets cold. But pretty soon there will be more snow, and then they'll all be skiing and working out that energy."

"I can't decide if I'm excited or nervous. Do I need chains?"

"Well, I'm not usually that kinky but if that's what you're into..." He fought his grin.

"Oh, you turd." Shiloh's laugh rang out, just warming the crisp, cold air. "I'll show you kinky."

"Will you?" He blushed, but he wasn't sure why. "So, chains are a no. What you need are snow tires, and if you have four-wheel or all-wheel drive, that would be good too."

"The truck has four-wheel drive. I used to go mudding with Matty quite a bit."

"Perfect." He squeezed Shiloh's arm. "You have to tell me more about him sometime. If you want to, I mean."

"He was a dork, wild and free, and addicted to the adrenaline rush."

"And you liked that about him..."

"I—I think I did, but I thought he was invincible. I thought we both were."

"You rode too?"

Shiloh stared at him, obviously shocked. "Oh, god no. I'm too tall, too clumsy, and I'm not a bull rider. Not at all."

"So if you didn't meet in the rodeo, how did you meet?" He pointed to the restaurant door and let go of Shiloh to open it.

"I was in college, and he was riding the rodeo in Austin. I was working at the bar, he walked in, and that was that. He spent the night at my apartment that first night."

That made Tate smile. "That's sweet. But I bet it was hard to be together."

"God yes. Everything about—" Shiloh stopped. "I shouldn't be talking about the rough parts."

They were seated and he opened his menu. "Why not?

It's not like any relationship is perfect. I'm listening. Talk about whatever you want."

"You don't think it's...mean-spirited?"

Whoa. Were they having a conversation?

"Why would it be? You're just talking about why it was hard to be together; you're not saying he was a bad person. You just said some really nice things about him. He had a job before he met you is all." It seemed like no one had ever asked Shiloh about Matty before. That was pretty sad too.

"He did. And he loved it more than life itself." Shiloh offered him a smile and rolled his eyes. "I swear, I thought it was so exciting. And every time he got hurt, it was a little less fun."

"I bet. Seems like a scary sport. It's dangerous, obviously. I can see why guys do it—adrenaline, money—but I couldn't. Did he ever talk about quitting?"

"Not once. He dreaded the idea of retiring." Shiloh chuckled and shook his head. "The thought of not riding made him nuts."

"Did you watch him ride in person a lot? I guess he was good, huh?"

"He was amazing—he never won a championship, but he won one finals event and a bunch of money." Shiloh snorted softly. "I tried it once—a practice bull. I broke my elbow. Everybody laughed, at least until they saw how bad it was."

Jesus. That sounded awful. "So how long were you together?"

"Nine years, give or take."

He couldn't help his surprise. "Oh wow. That's a long time." That was a lot to get over; no wonder Shiloh had been keeping to himself. "I've never been with anyone for...well,

I've never really had a real relationship. Just some short-term things."

"He was my first. I mean, like literally, my very first." Shiloh's cheeks went bright red, but he didn't look away for a second.

"That's pretty impressive, taking your very first home from a bar to your place." Tate grinned. "He was that hot, huh?"

"And he knew it. He never once doubted I wanted him. Not once."

"That kind of confidence is sexy." Shiloh had that confidence, maybe a little quieter, but when he knew he was wanted, he was hot as hell. He made sure to hold Shiloh's gaze. "Very sexy."

"Yes." Shiloh stared right into him. "And so is having someone who's being patient with your dorkitude."

"You're not... I mean, dork isn't the word I'd use. Maybe a little hesitant? But I guess it's been a while, so I get it."

The server interrupted long enough to get their orders and moved on. They both ordered steaks and they got some veggies to share.

"So how old were you when you decided you liked brussels sprouts? I was sixteen, and suddenly they were tasty."

Tate laughed. "I don't know. Maybe a year or two ago? I used to avoid them, actually, but then someone put some on my plate at some school function, and I felt obligated to at least try one. They were pretty good."

"Yeah. I don't care for them boiled, but roasted or fried, I'm so in."

"These were roasted and then tossed with some kind of dressing and served cold. They were good. I get them out a lot now. I love them warm and crunchy."

"Most things are better crunchy, babe." Shiloh winked at him.

He smiled back. "I don't know. I'm kind of a fan of soft and warm too."

"Yes. I missed that this week."

"I did too. I'm hoping you'll stay tonight?" Tonight, and any night Shiloh wanted to.

"I'd love that. Honestly. You've been on my mind, all week."

"Did you know you have this thing called a phone?" He grinned, teasing.

Shiloh's eyes went wide. "A-a-a *phone*?"

He rolled his eyes as their server set their drinks down. "Shut up. Just use it once in a while."

"I can do that. I wondered whether I should...but I didn't want to interrupt your week."

"You're not interrupting. You know where I am most nights." He shrugged. "And, to be fair, I wondered if I should, but I figured you were too tired to hang out."

"I was pretty tired, to be honest, but I would love to have been tired in your bed."

Hell, he was just going to say it. "Be tired in my bed next time. Any time. Your commute will be shorter." He laughed and sipped his beer.

"Very good to know." Shiloh lifted his wineglass and offered him a smile. "Things are starting to grow in the greenhouse. I'm very pleased."

"I can't wait to see. I poked my head in, but I didn't snoop. I want you to show me around." He touched his glass to Shiloh's. "To new things growing."

"Oh, I do like that. Very much. To new things growing." Shiloh took a deep, hard drink.

Tate watched his Adam's apple bob and all he could

think about was getting a kiss later. One of those long, deep kisses that made him forget his own name.

Shiloh put his glass down, then smiled at him. "Thank you for calling. It means a lot."

"Honestly, I couldn't take it anymore; I had to see you. I decided I'd rather you turn me down than keep wondering." That was about as truthful as he could be. He hoped it wasn't too much truth for Shiloh.

"I was—worried. I am...there's something about you that I like. A lot."

"I think I like everything about you, Shi. A lot."

Their steaks arrived, but not before he thought he caught a hint of a blush on the quiet cowboy.

He would remember this—how Shiloh was shockingly new to this whole love affair thing. How his cowboy would go for polite and careful every time. *His cowboy.* That seemed a little presumptuous at this point, but it was what he wanted, and he hadn't wanted anything as much in his whole life.

Plus, he'd seen the less polite and careful side of Shiloh and he was looking forward to seeing it again tonight.

15

Shiloh headed down to the greenhouse to check the progress of his little guys. It had snowed last night, like the weather had just been holding until he had spent the night again. It wasn't deep, just a dusting, but it was enough to make him smile.

He'd made biscuits and coffee, left Tate a note that he was down at the greenhouse. Then he took a plate of breakfast to Nash, said hi to the cows, and got busy. He loved how things were thriving, and he checked the pH levels on the soil and made sure the hydration levels were right.

Of all the places he could be and things he could be doing, this was a surprise. A greenhouse in Vermont, warm on the inside and surrounded by snow wasn't something he'd ever imagined for himself.

Still, it was interesting and fun. He was able to see total progress, and he loved to see the little green shoots coming up. Kale. Carrots. Onions. Mustard greens. Arugula. Even tomatoes.

His phone vibrated in his pocket, and he pulled it out to

find a text from Tate. There was a picture of Tate at the kitchen island, hair sticking up everywhere and smiling.

Biscuits are so good. Do you need more coffee?

Please. Want to come down and see?

He wanted to show off his work.

Yes. Need pants. Half a sec.

He chuckled. Pants were probably a good idea, given the snow and all.

Tate arrived a few minutes later in jeans, boots, and a big shearling-lined barn coat, carrying two insulated travel mugs. He'd even combed his hair. "Good morning. Ooh it's warm in here." Tate handed him a mug and unzipped his coat.

"It is. Welcome to your new garden!" He went over and took a long kiss, welcoming Tate in.

"There's a garden?" Tate asked playfully, a little breathless after their kiss.

"There's going to be, yes." He wrapped one arm around Tate and started showing off the plants. "I'm doing mostly winter greens, but I'm trying tomatoes. It would be amazing to have fresh ones in the winter."

"Oh, wow." Tate wandered with him, looking at everything. "This is amazing, Shi. Look at this place. Look, green things are growing. What are they?"

"That one's arugula. I'm pondering some starts of those native blackberries. You could sell them."

"Or you could sell them." Tate chuckled. "Arugula is

lettuce? I don't think I know one from another. That's embarrassing, huh?"

"It is. Yummy with parm and lemon. I love it. It's peppery."

"You'll have to make some for me when it comes in." Tate was curious, checking out all the different things he'd planted. "Are tomatoes hard?"

"I've never grown them here, and they're usually summer fruits, but...why not?" He wanted to try. He wanted to experiment.

"Cool. I like them." Tate leaned against him. "Thank you for breakfast. I can't believe I slept in. I must have been worn out."

"I hope so." His dick was raw, but it was so worth it.

Tate hummed. "Listen to you. Yes, you wore me out, cowboy. You're amazing."

"We're amazing together." And he was feeling like he was soaring about three inches off the ground.

"I know, right? Wow. And you cook, so I got super lucky." Tate kissed his cheek, then went to wander the greenhouse, looking at everything with interest.

"I'm growing carrots there. They aren't super happy yet."

"Oh, cool." Tate poked at the dirt gently. "How long do they take to show?"

"Around two weeks, give or take." He thought the cold might make it take longer, but he didn't know. This whole thing was an experiment.

"I'm so surprised it's not freezing in here. But I better make some rounds. Did you see Nash out there?"

He nodded. "I took him breakfast in the barn. He was milking."

"He works hard. Lots of farms around here have machines... I don't really want to get into that, so I only have what Nash can manage. I better go see if I can help. You want to come? I assume this isn't new to you."

"I've never milked, but the rest—I've done it, yeah. We ran beef cattle." And horses. Some goats.

"You're inspiring me to try cheese again. Maybe a simple farmer cheese to start." Tate smiled at him. "Button up; it's chilly out there."

"I'd totally help. Seriously." He could look it up. He'd made ricotta once, even.

He shrugged on his coat and zipped up.

"Cool. It's a plan." Tate led him out and toward the milking barn, where Nash had the little stove going in one corner, but it didn't do much for most of the barn. Still, inside was better than outside.

"Hey, bud."

"Hiya, Tate." Nash stood and wiped his hands off. "Thanks for the breakfast, Shiloh, that was unexpected and delicious."

"You're more than welcome. Happy Saturday." He didn't stand on ceremony, and folks needed feeding.

"Happier after those biscuits for sure."

"How's it going? You okay in the cold? You need some help?" Tate was watching Nash carefully.

"Well, I can use the hours if you need the time for something else."

Tate nodded. "Have at it, then. If you get cold, come in for a while and have some coffee, okay? And if you change your mind, we're here."

"Perfect. Thank you." Nash sat back down and got back to work.

Tate shrugged at him. "Looks like we're out of work."

"Want to go in and share another cup of coffee?" He wanted another kiss, and his feet were chilly.

"Sweet talker." Tate took his hand. "Are you used to snow?"

"Nope. This is my first where I wasn't traveling." He'd seen some before, sure, but this was the first living with it.

"We're getting a big storm in a couple of days. How about you get snowed in here with me?"

"I can't think of anything more fun." And romantic. And new. He loved the idea of new.

"Me either. They'll cancel classes, and we can watch the snow fall and stoke up the fire." Tate shrugged. "Well, and take care of the cows because Nash probably won't make it out here. He'll get the barn secured for the weather though; he's got a whole routine."

"I'm totally willing to help out. Should I run to the apartment and grab some clothes? Do I need to get groceries?"

"Probably a good idea. We could go together...if you want. If you're going to stay at my place I guess you should have some stuff here, huh?"

"I'd like that. I mean, if you don't mind. We can plan some meals even?" God, this was a delicate walk—the dance between saying he was in and not looking like a stalker.

"Sounds great. And we can get whatever snacks you like. I have this great smoker out back now, did you know?" Tate leaned on him.

"I did know. We could smoke a turkey in a few weeks. They'll be on sale." He did love a smoked bird.

"How do you even know that? I'm the wander in and buy stuff that looks good type. I bet you even make a *list*."

He rolled his eyes and grinned. "I used to. We lived an hour from the closest grocery, so I planned. Here, it's easier."

"Well, it's a small grocery, but it's a good one. So do you need a list, or should we just get going?"

"Let's just go." He stole a kiss. "I'll grab my toothbrush and phone charger, and you can see my apartment."

It was little and a bit shabby, but clean and perfect for walking around downtown.

"You might want clothes. Maybe socks..." Tate followed him out and they climbed into his truck.

"I like socks. Skyler's Charlie apparently wants me to buy better socks." She had put them on his Christmas list. She was a little—a lot—early.

"Charlie is that age where she has opinions. I saw them on her face when she arrived for the barbeque."

"Yeah? I guess so. She's a neat kid, and the little ones? Make me laugh so hard." He was fascinated by the ways their brains worked—how they started making jokes, learning from Charlie, using language.

"I know she's adopted, but she reminds me of Sky. She seems just like him. Only with pre-tween attitude." Tate chuckled. "I wouldn't have put Sky and Beckett together, but they're great parents."

"No one was betting on them early on in their marriage either, trust me." In fact, they'd been either divorced or damn near when Sky had his bad wreck.

Tate looked out the window, then glanced around his truck. "It's weird to be in the passenger seat."

"Yeah? You drive a lot, huh?" Deliveries and back and forth to the school.

"All the time. My truck, the delivery truck. Mostly the milk gets picked up, but sometimes I drive that too. And I like being in town, which is a drive, obviously. Someday the farm will be self-sustaining; that's the goal. Then I won't need the second job."

"The greenhouse will help that. You can sell fresh vegetables and fruits, plus plant starts in the spring." In fact, he could see this being a nice boost to Tate's coffers. He loved the idea of a farm stand—something with pumpkins in the fall and tomatoes in the summer.

Tate nodded. "Yeah? We could have quite the little business, huh?"

"Totally. If your goal is to be self-sufficient, this is one way to do it. I'm a big fan of creating income while doing right for the earth."

"I'm in. It sounds great. We can build the stand when the snow thaws. There's not a lot else to do during mud season."

"There's a mud season? Do you go mudding?" That was always fun.

"Um. No?" Tate looked confused.

"Oh. No, because it's awful or no, because you don't know it?"

Tate grinned. "I don't know what it is. Is it like snowshoeing in the mud? We mostly avoid the mud around here."

"It's driving your truck in the mud and throwing it everywhere. In Texas, this is a huge weekend thing."

Tate laughed. "Really? I think maybe we're too mountainy for that? Too many trees maybe?"

"Could be. Where I'm from, there's not many mountains. At all." He winked over, teasing. "I'll find you YouTube videos. You'll cackle."

"I bet." They rolled into town, which was busy with shoppers, dog walkers, and people out running errands. "Wow. I'm hardly ever here this early in the day."

"Oh, yeah? I am out this time quite a bit, weirdly." He loved being among the people, because it had made him feel less like a ghost. Now, he knew he wasn't.

"I try to help Nash on the weekends, mostly for the company. But lately he's really been wanting the money, so

I've been letting him work, you know? So I'm in town in the evenings more."

"It's good to have a hand that wants to work, right? That's important."

Tate shook his head. "It's a weird thing. I'm working the second job mostly to pay him because I need someone to be here working when I have to be at school. It made sense to me at first, but now that he wants to do more..."

"Man, that is tough." That sucked, to work a second job to pay another dude. He didn't even know how to address it, because no way he offered to help seemed like it would actually do anything.

"It'll shake out. I need him and he needs me, right? I could quit teaching, but I love it."

"No. No, I can see that. I think teachers are important as all get out. I know it doesn't feel like I'm into education and stuff, but I totally am." He had his degree, and he loved learning.

"Hey, you're into something very important too. The earth, growing things. Cooking, too. Feeding people. I think that's pretty cool." They pulled into a little parking lot behind a row of shops.

"I do too. I love the idea of growing things that make food, teas, medicine—it's amazing. It feels like... It feels like I'm part of nature, somehow." And that probably sounded dumb, but it was how he felt.

"That's your calling. The earth, dirt, nurturing things. I get it; teaching is nurturing too. I just help minds grow." Tate got out of the truck and followed him, one hand sliding into his.

"Right on. I want to help the farm grow, so you don't have to work another job." He meant it, too. Tate was a good man, and he deserved his own time.

"Well, we'll see what we can do. Is this where you live? This close to the bar? Wow."

"I do. It's on the second floor. It's not meant to be forever, but it's clean and decent, you know?" He led Tate upstairs and unlocked the door, letting him in.

It had come furnished, so really the only thing he'd had to buy was the kitchen stuff and his TV. Easy-peasy. It was a studio, and he kept it simple. His comforter was a deep, rich maroon, and there was a single photo of him and Matty together, laughing on the day they got married.

"Most of these little places in town are nice. Small, like this one, but nice." Tate glanced around, headed straight for the picture and picked it up. "This is a great picture. Look how happy you are. He had that rugged handsome thing going on."

"I was happy." Shiloh had been. He'd loved Matty to distraction, but instead of hurting, he found himself smiling. He had loved that wild bastard to death. "He would have adored you."

"Me? You think so? I don't know what a bull rider would like about me. I'm boring. Steady, maybe, but boring."

"He didn't like other bull riders, honey. Me? I'm a botanist. I cook. I'm not an adrenaline junkie." He was steady and boring too, but he grew things, he made things. That wasn't bad. "Matty loved that. There was a part of him that was jealous of it."

"I think I would have liked him too. I'm sure I would, since he obviously loved you."

"He did, and it was a wild ride." He wrapped one arm around Tate's waist, daring to kiss Tate's cheek. "I don't think about him, you know? When we're making love. I was terrified I would, but I don't."

"I hadn't thought about that." Tate set the picture down

and caught his gaze, searching. "I guess that means you're ready for me."

"I guess it does." He held Tate's eyes, letting himself breathe with that for a nice, long minute. "Are you ready for me?"

"Oh." Tate leaned into him a little. "I think so. I hope so. I don't know. How do I know?"

"We just trust each other, and we learn all about each other?" That was at least a solid answer.

"That's easy." Tate kissed his cheek and sat on the bed. "Do you need help packing?"

"I'd like that." He chuckled softly and went to pull out a suitcase. "You can help me decide how long the snow is going to last."

16

"Happy Halloween, Mr. Dutton!"

"Who's under there?" Tate squinted at Darth Vader.

Darth lifted his mask. "Pete."

"Whoa, Pete! Good to see you. Did you enjoy the parade?"

"It was okay, my little sisters loved it, so...that was good. Time for candy."

It never ceased to amaze him how teenagers were so unimpressed by everything. "Well, have fun. Happy Halloween."

Pete jogged off to join his family and Tate took Shiloh's hand. "What did *you* think of the parade?"

"I thought it was adorable. Did you see little Sierra? That was the cutest bumblebee ever! And Noah as a puppy?" Shiloh was all grins. "And then there was the Unicowgirl and her daddy, Unicowboy."

"I love this parade; it's always wild."

"Hey, man. Hey, Shiloh." Kent gave a wave and headed his way. Josh and Zeke were with him.

"Hey, what's up?" Tate shook their hands.

"We haven't seen you guys at the bar lately, everything okay?"

Was it okay?

He'd never been so warm at night, he'd never eaten so well, and he'd never learned more about plants.

"Everything's great. Shiloh built a greenhouse, and we've been working on a farm stand...just busy. We'll come this weekend though."

"Come tonight, it's Halloween. It'll be fun."

Tate glanced at Shiloh. It had been a while. "Yeah? Maybe, yeah."

Shiloh smiled, and it didn't look stressed. "Totally up to you. I could have a sip of whiskey before we head home."

"Okay, sounds great."

"Right on." Josh clapped Shiloh on the shoulder. "We'll see you guys there."

"This has been so fun, but man, it's cold!" Shiloh wasn't complaining. He was laughing, happy, bundled up and excited.

"You better get used it because it only gets colder, cowboy." He laughed. "Oh, that's Bryn. Bri!" He waved a hand and she smiled and jogged over.

"Hi, Tate! Did you watch the parade? Oh, are you here with—" Bryn turned right to Shiloh. "Are you Shiloh? Wow. You're even better looking than Tate said."

"I am Shiloh. And thank you. I came out the lucky one." Shiloh held out one hand to shake. "Pleased to meet you, ma'am."

"I'm Bryn. Tate talks about you all the time."

"Bryn..." Tate shook his head.

"He says you've basically moved in, huh? Lucky man."

Shiloh blushed bright red. "I—well, I still pay for an apartment, but...well, you can find me there."

"Hey, we gotta run, Bri. Happy Halloween."

"Oh, sure. Have fun guys. See you Monday, Tate."

Tate snorted and tugged Shiloh toward the bar. "Sorry about that. She's a...a work friend."

"She's nice. You talk about me at work?"

"I talk about you with my friends. She's a friend." Was that a bad thing?

"That's cool. Matt and I had to be careful, you know? Not scared, but careful."

Oh, right. He hadn't even thought of that. "Not cool to be out in the rodeo, I guess. I don't think there's anyone I know that doesn't know who I am. I guess that will take some getting used to for you? Vermont is super chill that way. People are people."

"It's new, and that makes it a little special. There's still a little rush."

He liked the idea of being able to give Shiloh something new. "Then I'm going to show you off every chance I get."

Shiloh blushed and squeezed his hand. "I bought us a bag of Reese's, so we could celebrate tonight."

"You did? That is so sweet." So adorable. Shiloh could be so serious, but then do little things like that. He loved it. "Chocolate and peanut butter taste better naked, you know."

"I've heard that, believe it or not." Shiloh waggled his eyebrows. "It's like body shots, if you use the minis."

"Oh, I'm so in." He laughed. They wandered into the bar, which was louder and more crowded than usual. Kent and Josh were even dancing to the Monster Mash on the pool table. "Look at that," he grinned, dragging Shiloh farther inside.

"Oh, wow. They fall, that's going to hurt." Shiloh dropped his voice. "And I would laugh like anything."

"You're evil." Tate laughed. "I would too. Buy me a drink?"

"I'd be honored. You'd like a beer?" Shiloh kissed his hand, and Tate grinned, because how daring did that have to feel?

"I would, please." He would push Shiloh a little in private, but in public, he let Shiloh drive, so that kiss was even more important to him. He sat and let Shiloh do the ordering, feeling like a very lucky date.

Shiloh came over with his beer and a whiskey. His lover hadn't been lying when he said he didn't care for beer. Could cowboys not like beer?

"Thank you." He took a sip as soon as Shiloh handed it to him. "So, I have to ask...what don't you like about beer?"

"I think it's bitter and sour. I like cooking with it, but—" Shiloh wrinkled his nose. "I just can't handle it."

"Well, at least we can compromise on wine." The music changed, and he noticed a little dance floor that wasn't usually there. They must have moved some tables to make room.

"Hey, guys, you made it!" Zeke dragged a chair over and sat down. "Mind if I get off my feet a second? Thanks."

"Did the parade wear you out?"

"Haha. The whole thing can't be more than eight or ten blocks long." Zeke started emptying his pockets of sweets.

Shiloh snorted softly. "Did you get yourself enough candy on the way?"

"Is there such a thing as enough candy?" Zeke pushed some over to Shiloh. "You look like a 3 Musketeers guy to me."

Shiloh shot Tate a teasing, loving glance. "Do I now?"

"Tate is a Snickers man." Zeke pushed one toward him and he took it and ripped it open. "Hell, yeah."

"Peanuts and caramel and chocolate. There's no bad there." Shiloh ate the little candy bar, then had a sip of whiskey.

"Right? Of all the people to finally catch Tate's eye, it had to be a 3 Musketeers man." Zeke laughed. "We all thought he'd be single forever."

"That would have been a terrible shame." Shiloh winked at Zeke, then smiled at Tate. "I couldn't let that happen."

"Oh, no? Good thing I decided to talk to you then, huh?" Tate teased him. "Before they engraved your name on that booth."

"Don't you have to sit in the same seat for five years before that happens?"

Zeke laughed and pushed back from their table. "Enjoy the chocolate."

"Thanks, man. We'll buy you a drink later."

"Yeah? Awesome!" Zeke pushed his chair back in and bounced away.

"Couldn't let that happen, huh?" He leaned toward Shiloh.

"I couldn't, no. You were determined and fine, and I didn't want to say no."

Tate took his hand. "I hope you never do."

Shiloh held on, watching him, and time seemed to stretch.

"Tate! Shiloh! Come dance!" someone shouted.

He wasn't ready to break that gaze, but he did blink a couple of times before looking away. It was Kent who'd shouted, this time from the dance floor, which seemed safer than the pool table.

"Do you want to dance?"

"Sure. I'm not good at it, but it's fun anyway."

"I'm not either. Fun is the point." He stood up and tugged Shiloh out of his chair. The tiny dance floor had a few people on it, but it wasn't packed. The weird Halloween music wasn't the easiest to dance to, not the way he wanted to dance anyway, but he tried to make the best of it.

Shiloh was a great sport, shaking his butt and making everyone laugh.

He reached for that amazing ass and caught one denim-clad cheek, giving it a quick squeeze, enjoying everything about their evening so far. "Looking good, cowboy."

"Am I? I'm working off my candy bars."

"You've got some moves, baby." They looked like fools, the two of them, but he didn't even care. He couldn't remember the last time he'd had so much fun.

"Yeah. I'm like Patrick Swayze." That set all of them off, the laughter filling the air.

"Come here, loverboy." He pulled Shiloh in by the front of his shirt.

"Ooh... I do like a man who loves his classics." Shiloh's hand landed on his hip.

"Are you a classic?" He teased, trying to bait his man into a kiss.

"Dude. I'm pretty sure I'm not even vintage yet."

He danced close, one arm around Shiloh's back. "No, you're not vintage. You're the real deal though."

"So are you. I—" Shiloh's phone started to ring, and he frowned. "You mind if I check?"

"Of course not." He followed Shiloh off the dance floor.

"Hey man, what's—Okay, what do you need? Of course. Of course, man. I'll be there in ten. No problem at all." Shiloh hung up and met his eyes. "Sky. Charlie jumped off the porch. They think her leg's broke. Nanny's gone to visit family. They need me to watch the others." Shiloh headed for the booth for his coat and hat, before looking over his shoulder. "You coming, honey?"

"You know it."

"Hey, you guys! Where are you—"

He waved Kent off. "Family emergency. I'll text you later!" He scooped up his coat and followed without missing a beat. "She was just at the parade. That's crazy."

"Yeah. She's a wild one, I guess. Beck's heading to the ER with her, and Sky will follow when we get to theirs."

"Poor kid. After everything they did with the greenhouse, I'm happy to help out."

"I appreciate it. They'll be asleep in a few heartbeats, I bet. Poor Charlie... I hate thinking she's hurting." Shiloh was almost running now.

He kept up, basically jogging himself, until they got to Shiloh's truck. Shiloh had been driving them almost everywhere lately. "You okay? Do you want me to drive?"

"I'm good. I got this. I think I do anyway." Shiloh winked at him. "Here we go to the rescue!"

"Uncle Shiloh in shining armor." Tate pulled on his seatbelt.

"Uncle Shiloh and Tate. That's important."

That was so sweet it made his cheeks heat up and he slid a hand over Shiloh's thigh. "I think we're important. Yes."

"Yeah. Me too." They headed out of town, moving out past their turn, past the city lights.

"That was fun, right? Dancing and hanging out with people. My friends? You looked like you were having fun." Shiloh wasn't the party type he didn't think, but he was a good sport. And Tate wanted Shiloh to like his friends, and maybe to make some new ones together.

"It was. I was having a ball." Shiloh didn't sound like he was bullshitting him at all. "We should dance more often."

"We should. I was really enjoying that. You. So much." He squeezed Shiloh's thigh gently. He smiled at Shiloh but wasn't sure Shiloh could see in the dark cab of the truck. "We'll have to send some flowers or something for Charlie tomorrow."

"Totally. You think they'll keep her?"

"I guess it depends. Hopefully not, right? But she might be stuck at home for a few days. They'd brighten up her room."

"Totally, and I bet she's never had anyone send her flowers before." Shiloh shook his head and sighed softly. "I always thought that was the most romantic gesture ever— getting flowers. Stupid, I know, but true."

"It's not stupid." He filed that away for another day. "Did Matty bring you flowers a lot?"

"No. The day we got married. There weren't flowers for the ceremony, but I went out and the truck was filled with yellow roses."

That made him smile. "Oh, that's so sweet. I can just picture it. That's love."

"It was. It was silly and romantic and weirdly Matty. He wouldn't be thoughtful for months and months, and then he'd shock me with something."

"There's no right way to love someone I guess." He watched the house grow closer as Shiloh pulled into the drive. It was lit up like they were having a party. Every outside light was on, most of the rooms warm and bright inside.

"Okay. Let's go in and let that man get to his eldest." Shiloh stole a quick, hard kiss. "Thank you."

"You can stop thanking me now." He grinned and slid

out of the truck. His truck was smaller and older, and he could get out easily. Shiloh's truck was a monster by comparison.

Sky was pacing on the front porch, Sierra sobbing on the top step in the cold, the little one hysterical. "Y'all. Thank god. I need to go. She's melting down."

"M' not!"

"Girl!"

The wailing got louder.

Tate reached for Sierra, she pulled away, and poor Sky looked frantic. "I'm crazy good with kids. I'm a teacher. Kids love me. We've got her, you go."

Sky gave Tate a grateful smile. "Thanks. I'll call. Noah's already out. Sound asleep. Talk to you soon."

Then Sky was off like a shot, running for his truck.

"This is kind of scary, huh?" He sat beside Sierra, keeping his hands to himself this time.

Sierra glanced at him and nodded, sniffling.

"Charlie's going to be okay. I broke my leg when I was a little older than she is, and I healed up good as new."

"I didn't do it. I didn't push her." She sniffled hard.

Oh, man. "Did she say you pushed her?"

"No! No, but I wanted to do it too, and I falled back, and she falled that way!"

Shiloh's lips twisted, and he leaned. "Oh, lord, little chick. Y'all shouldn't be trying to fly, either one of you."

"It was an accident; nobody thinks you pushed her. How about we go inside, and I make you something to drink? It's late, you should probably head to bed. I bet Uncle Shiloh would read to you."

"Is she gonna die?"

"Little chick, your sister is a cowboy. She's going to heal right up. C'mere." Shiloh held his arms open, and Sierra ran to him. "Lord have mercy, you have had a busy Halloween."

"I have a lot of candy, but Pappy took it. He said only two a day." Sierra snuggled in hard.

"Well, that means you get candy for so many days! How neat is that?"

She frowned, and then she grinned. "Oh. So lots of days?"

"That's right! That's like Halloween over and over."

Shiloh was so good with her. He followed them inside, and stayed out of the way while Shiloh got her ready for bed. He didn't even try to field all her questions. And she had a lot of them.

"When is Charlie coming home?"

"When the doctors help her leg."

"Can I talk to Pappy?"

"Not right now."

"Can I sleep with Noah?"

"Little chick, he's already asleep." Shiloh was so patient.

Sierra sighed. "How do you walk with a broken leg?"

"It depends on how badly she broke it. She might have crutches. How about I read to you? You pick the book."

"Doozer book?"

"Sure. Grab it." Shiloh glanced at him and mouthed, "Coffee?"

He nodded and looked at Sierra. "You sleep well. Goodnight." He gave Shiloh a wink and went downstairs to find the coffee maker.

Coffee was a good idea. He found Sky and Beckett's stash and made a strong pot, figuring they were going to be up pretty late.

The house here was way less fancy than the outside said it would be. Inside it was filled with toys and books and blankets and a huge cat tree. And just as he was about to go sit near the wood stove to wait for the coffee to brew, a big dog lifted his head from the couch cushions.

"Hey there." The dog's tail started to wag, slapping against the couch, so he went over and sat. "What's your name?" He reached for the dog's collar, it said "Bruiser" on the tag. Bruiser shifted forward and his big head landed in Tate's lap. "How am I going to pour Shiloh a cup of coffee with you leaning on me?"

Bruiser woofed softly, like he was answering straight away, like he understood what Tate was saying.

He gave Bruiser a good scritch. He loved dogs; he just wasn't home enough to have one. "Oh, you like that do you? Who's a good boy? Such a pretty pup." He wasn't sure what to do with the cat that was pacing back and forth on the back of the couch, though.

Every time he met the kitty's eyes, it made this terribly unfriendly sound.

Geez. "Kitty doesn't like me, Bruiser." He glanced toward the kitchen. Poor Sierra must have been wired. Shiloh had to be on book three by now.

"She's out. Hey, Walter." Shiloh went to the kitchen and pulled out mugs.

"Is that his name? Bruiser loves me. The cat? Not so much. I'd get up to help, but..." He gave Shiloh a helpless smile.

"Walter hates everyone but Sierra." Shiloh rolled his eyes. "Sky used to travel with Walter in his trailer."

"He's looking a little white around the whiskers, so I'll forgive him for being grumpy."

"Oh, he was found grumpy. Sky rescued him from the bull pens somewhere, and that cat was determined no one would ever hurt him again." Shiloh chuckled.

"Well, he's got a pretty sweet setup. Look at that cat tree. Big step up from bull pens, I bet. I love how homey it is in here."

"It is." Shiloh brought him a cup of coffee and came to sit next to him. "It feels like people that love each other live here."

He couldn't help his smile. "Right? Warm. They'd probably apologize for the mess. I'd just ask if they were having fun."

"Yeah. No mess means someone's not making something, or that's what my granny used to say."

He took Shiloh's hand. "You're good with her. Sierra. She trusts you. You like kids?"

"I love them, yes. I don't have to ask you whether you care for them."

He chuckled. "I work with teenagers, but I like the younger kids too. They're so...honest. They just are who they are." He glanced at Shiloh. "I could totally do the dad thing."

"Yeah. Yeah, me too. I want—I wanted—I mean, it's like a pipe dream for gay guys in a lot of ways, and then you find couples like Sky and Beck."

"It can happen if...you..." Jesus, he almost said "we". "It's not so rare anymore at all."

"Yeah?" Shiloh smiled, and the expression was like seeing the sun rise. "That's good to know."

"Right?" His ears and his cheeks warmed, and he knew he was blushing, which only made them heat up more.

"Yeah. Yeah, right." They stared at each other, then they started chuckling, laughing softly at their goofiness.

He shook his head. "How about you kiss me?" He leaned in knowing the answer would be yes.

And it was. A most resounding yes.

17

Shiloh slogged through the snow to the greenhouse, needing to check all his growing beauties. The world in that little space was magical—fecund and rich, full of growth. He was happy in there, testing different seedlings, different nutrients.

He harvested some spinach and some kale, and then peered at his lemon seedlings. He wanted to grow some lemon and lime trees for the house, for cooking and for the joy of green in the house.

Tate hadn't even blinked at the six inches of new snow they'd gotten overnight; he'd just made his coffee like always, brushed off his truck and headed off to school. Nash was in the barn like usual, too. Snow didn't seem to slow anyone down up here.

It freaked him out a little, but it was slowly becoming normal.

Especially now that he was spending the night with Tate more often than not...

He kept things in the bathroom. He had a dresser in the bedroom. Tate had let him put up a hook for his hat by the front door. Things were moving in a moving-in direction. Quickly.

It was weird, but not. Tate seemed like he was welcome, like he was meant to be here, and Shiloh wanted to believe in it. He'd believed in Matty, and that had been magic, for as long as he had it.

His phone chimed and he pulled it out of his pocket. Tate had sent him a picture of a snow drift at the high school as tall as his truck followed by a bunch of goofy laughing emojis. He shook his head and was just about to text back when there was a knock on the greenhouse door.

Who knocked on the door to a greenhouse?

"Uh, Shiloh? Sorry to bug you, man. You got a minute?"

Nash apparently knocked on a greenhouse door.

"Sure. I was just puttering around in here." He went to the door, following Nash when he headed out into the snow.

"I tried to call Tate, but I know the cell service over there is spotty, or I guess he might be in class. I wanted another opinion. I think we need to call the vet."

"Oh no. One of the cows?" He had no idea, but he'd seen a lot of cattle in his life. He could guess.

"Nope. Not a cow. A dog. Some kind of shepherd mix. I found her on the back porch and brought her in out of the weather. I think she might be pregnant?" Nash led him into the barn and pulled back the door on the very first stall.

"Oh man." That he knew about. "I've had a few dogs in my life."

Shiloh knelt down in front of the mama dog, giving her some space. "Hey, girl. How are you doing?"

This stall worked as a whelping box, but he had a wooden box that he could put some old towels in that would be cozy.

The dog barely lifted her head, just sighing at him.

"She seems so tired, doesn't she? I didn't see a collar so I have no idea who she could belong to."

"Okay. Let me get her water and a whelping box. Can you call the vet? I'll pay for it, okay?" He didn't wait for Nash to answer. He took off like a bat out of hell.

He pulled one of the extra boxes from the greenhouse, plus a bunch of old towels from the house before jogging back.

"You need some help?" Nash hovered nervously. "The vet's sending someone, but it might be a couple of hours."

"I'm going to get her warm and comfy and safe. She's a sweetheart, aren't you, Mama?"

"Is it warm enough out here for her? For the pups? I almost put her in the house, but I thought Tate might not be so happy with that."

"Let's take her in. I'll take the blame. If he fusses, it's all on me." He wouldn't have her freezing.

Nash nodded. "I can carry her; she let me get her in here. You want to wrap her in one of your towels?" Nash stepped right in to help.

"Totally." He handed the towels over, hating how listless she was.

They got her wrapped up and he brought the box while Nash carried her to the house. "Where should we put her?"

"Let's put her in the laundry room. It's cozy and tiled." He got her set up, a bowl of water close. "She probably won't eat. Is there dog food anywhere?"

"I don't think so. I could make a run."

"Please. Get the good stuff, canned and dry." He pulled out some cash. "Plus bowls for food and water."

She'd already sucked down half of a bowl.

Nash put the cash in his pocket. "Got it. I'll be back soon. Should I keep trying Tate, or have you got that?"

"I'll call him on his free period." He had Tate's schedule down. He left the laundry room door open and started doing normal shit, so Mama dog could relax.

Nash left, and the house was quiet for an hour or so before the vet showed up, and she was very nice, but she didn't tell him anything he didn't already know. "She's ready to go, no more than forty-eight hours I don't think. Could even be tonight. I'm going to give you a course of antibiotics for her and also some salve for that cut on her leg. Can someone stay here with her?"

"I'm right here. The puppies sound alive then?" That had been his biggest worry—that those pups were rotting inside her.

"They do, there's good movement, and there are a lot of them. Maybe ten. Or a dozen. I can't say they'll all survive, but many will. You can call me if you need help and I'll come back." She handed him her business card. "I'm on call tonight."

"Me too." He winked at her, then texted Tate.

> Call me when you can, babe?

Tate came back quickly with,

> Yep, let me step out

"Hey, you. We got a situation. I'm handling it, but I wanted you to be aware. Nash found a pregnant mama dog in the barns. I've got her in the laundry room." He got it out in a single breath.

"Really? Wow. Okay...is she okay? Did she have a tag? We can take her home later."

"She's in bad shape. She's hungry and skinny. No tag. No

chip." And if she had an owner, they hadn't been doing right by her.

"Nash has the number for the vet. They would probably board her until she has the puppies." Tate sounded like he was being practical, not mad.

"Oh, honey. These puppies are imminent. I've got it. The vet's seen them, and she's good here. I mean... I can take her to the apartment if you'd rather, but..." But he didn't want to. He sort of wanted this to be part of the memories Tate and he were making.

"Oh. Well, no. No, don't move her then, poor thing. It sounds like you know what you're doing, so I'll...see her when I get home. It's fine."

Did it sound fine? He wasn't sure.

"Is stew good for supper? I'll make garlic bread." Was he bribing his lover with food?

"You make the best garlic bread. Sounds great. Thank you." He could almost hear Tate's smile. Bribery, peace offering, whatever it was, it worked.

They hung up, and he got to his feet. "Okay, little sister. I'm going to talk and cook. I'm here if you need support." He started making the garlic knots that made Tate happy.

18

It had been snowing all day, and Tate had been a teacher long enough to know a looming snow day when he saw one. No need for a spoon under his pillow or to wear his pajamas inside out tonight.

Come to that, he was hoping not to be wearing pajamas at all to bed tonight.

He slid out of his truck and grabbed all the grading he'd brought home with him so he could take advantage of the day off and trudged into the mud room. "Hey, baby," he called out while he shrugged out of his snowy coat and wet boots. "How's momma doggo?"

"Annabelle is on puppy three. She's doing good. How are you, honey?"

"Fine. Wet. It's snowy out there. Pretty sure school will be closed tomorrow." He answered as he made his way to the laundry room. He kissed the top of Shiloh's head when he got there. The room was too small for both of them to sit so he hung out in the doorway. "You named her Annabelle? Wow, she looks exhausted. Three of how many?"

"Doc didn't know. We'll just have to see. She's a shepherd mix, but these are fuzzy black and white critters."

"They're so small. Are they okay?" He crouched down to get a better look.

The mama dog gave him a worried glance, and Shiloh balanced him. "Seem to be. We'll get the vet out in a day or two to make sure all is well."

"Are you hungry? Do you want me to make something you can eat in here?"

"No. No, I'll just peek in on her. There's stew in the slow cooker for us."

"I've been looking forward to it." He offered Shiloh a hand up. "I brought home some of those cookies you like from the bakery and a loaf of sourdough. They were practically giving things away. I think they plan to be closed tomorrow morning."

"Oh, damn. Is it snowing that hard?" Right, this was Shiloh's first big dumping.

"Not all that hard, but it's been snowing all day, and it doesn't look like it's going to stop any time soon. Wait until you see the property in the morning with all the snow...and the barn. I don't know if Nash will make it up here though so we may have some work to do."

"Good thing I'm not scared of working, honey." Shiloh's grin was pure tease, all laughter. "Hey, I'm glad you're home."

He leaned into Shiloh and kissed his chin. "Me too. You're warm. Snow is not."

"I've never had a snow day before. Is it cool to be excited?"

"It's cool. All my kids are. And I do love a snow day. After we do our chores we can snuggle by the fire and watch movies while I grade papers."

"Sounds perfect, and there will be puppies." Shiloh gave him the big eyes. "She seems like she's done this before. She cleaned the first ones right up."

"Oh, good. I hope it's not too long a night for her."

"You and me both, honey. I want her to get through this with flying colors."

"Are you going to call someone after the snowstorm? A... shelter maybe?"

"If I can find a rescue, I'll see what I can do. She's young to be such a good mom. She'll need to be fixed."

"Sure. That makes sense. Oh, the stew smells too good." Tate got down two wide, shallow bowls and set them out. "Mind if I have a beer?"

"I'll have a drink with you. There's bread—garlic knots for the win."

"Oh, yum. You're amazing. You did all that while dealing with the dog... I'm impressed." He set a glass out for Shiloh and sat the bottle of whiskey beside it before digging in the fridge for his beer.

"Dogs are easy, mostly. I grew up with them. Hell, I sold the ranch after my last girl—Pepper—died."

"Aww. What kind of dog was Pepper?" He opened his beer, then poured Shiloh a finger of whiskey.

"Part pit bull, part Aussie, part hippopotamus." Shiloh managed to say that with a straight face. Impressive.

He couldn't keep in his own laughter at all. "So...big?"

"Massive. Like a tank. She cracked me up." Shiloh grabbed his phone and showed off a picture of a black and white beast with a huge, slobbery grin. "That's my little girl."

"Look at that face." Little she was not. He could see how Shiloh was in love with her though. He set his beer down on the counter as something dawned on him. Shiloh was already in love with this one. "You want to keep her, don't you?"

"Huh?" Shiloh's eyes went wide, and his cheeks went red. "I wouldn't make that sort of decision without talking to you. I mean, my apartment is awful small for dogs."

He'd never get over how beautiful Shiloh was when he blushed. Or the fact that Shiloh blushed at all. "You mean the apartment you haven't been to in weeks?" As far as he was concerned, Shiloh had moved in. And who could say no to that look? "We can keep her here. There's plenty of room for a dog, and she can keep Nash company too."

"Yeah, that apartment—" Shiloh grinned at him. "If I stopped paying for that, I could put that cash into covering bills and stuff here. Maybe you could just work one job, even."

"Why, Shiloh, are you asking to move in with me?" He gave his lover a playful look. It was a big step, but one he'd already thought about. He'd been waiting, trying to be respectful. It was an even bigger step for Shiloh after all— deciding if he, and if Vermont, was where he wanted to call home now.

"I—" Shiloh took a deep breath, held his eyes, and nodded. "I am. I'm wasting money on a place I don't go to. You're working two jobs when you don't have to. Not to mention, I've got a side of a bed and a place on the sofa."

"Well that all sounds very practical." He moved around the counter and circled his arms around Shiloh. "I love you. You don't have to say it back yet, but that's how I feel. I want to live together."

"Then that makes us very even." Shiloh stepped right in and took a kiss that felt very much like a promise.

Tate dove right into it, holding on tight. He'd take that

promise and hold Shiloh to it. People said talking was important, but Shiloh didn't always need words to explain himself. Tate's cowboy seemed very clear in his actions, his touches, his kisses.

He was ready to leave the stew on warm and see where this moment took them until Annabelle whined from the laundry room. He and Shiloh both froze. "You need to check on her?"

"Yeah. Yeah, I'll be right back." Shiloh kissed his nose and headed for the laundry room. "How you doing, Momma? Oh, two more. You're doing so good."

"Two more?" He followed Shiloh so he could see them. They were so tiny. How something so small grew into a big dog like Annabelle was beyond him. "Wow. She's going to have her paws full."

"Yeah. I hope there aren't a ton more. She's getting tired." Shiloh stayed close, but he didn't touch her at all.

How many more could there be?

"Well, there can't be a ton more, can there?"

"I've seen litters of fourteen..."

"No way, really? Fourteen. Wow." He watched the poor dog; she really did look tired. "Does she need anything? What happens if she's too tired to finish this by herself?"

"We call the vet. She'll go septic if they die inside her."

"Geez. So we need to check on her all night, huh?" Good thing they could nap all they wanted tomorrow. "I hope the vet can get here with the weather."

"Well, let's hope that we won't need her. That's better, right?"

"That's better. Of course." He wasn't sure what to do now. "You think she's okay? Should we go try to eat again? Your garlic knots are making me hungry."

"Let's eat. She'll let us know if she needs us." Shiloh gave him a hopeful grin. "I'm starving."

"Plus, we were having a moment." He winked and gave Shiloh a hand up.

"I like our moments. A lot." Shiloh stood and cupped his cock in one smooth move.

"Jesus, me too." He leaned into the touch, torn between garlic knots and taking Shiloh right to bed. "Especially the long ones."

"Mmhmm...you know all about long..."

"If you're trying to seduce me, Mr. Shiloh, it's working." He begged a kiss, and tucked his hands into Shiloh's back pockets, getting a little taste of that amazing ass.

Shiloh took his mouth, the kiss sudden and hungry, that fine butt firm and tight under his fingers.

He loved the way they could turn each other on—this solid, stoic hunk of cowboy was totally his whenever he wanted, and he was putty in his lover's hands. He moaned and pushed their hips together, helpless to that amazing kiss, opening to accept an impatient tongue.

Shiloh backed him up to the kitchen counter, moving him until he didn't have anywhere to go before rocking into him and making him moan. He scrambled for something to give him some leverage and ended up bracing himself on either side, fingers curling around the edge of the countertop.

"So fucking pretty," Shiloh rumbled, cock stiff and heavy against him, through both layers of clothes.

"You make my knees weak, Shi, I swear." He was burning up; his balls ached, and there wasn't much he could do about it, pinned as he was. "You feel so good."

"Mmhmm." Shiloh bit his bottom lip and groaned, hands like iron bands where they wrapped around his hips.

He let go of the counter and tugged at Shiloh's shirt, working his hands up underneath it to touch skin, explore the hard abs. "Please. Take whatever you want. I need you."

"Take your cock out. I want to see."

Shiloh's tone stole his breath. "You better back up then, cowboy. I can't even move the way you're on me."

"Dammit. I can't have it both ways?" Shiloh eased back —almost enough for him to move.

"You can have it any way you want, baby." He sighed as he squeezed a hand between them and fished out his cock, the heat from his own fingers making him moan. "Can I have yours?"

"You can have every fucking thing I have." That sounded like a promise.

"That's what I want. Every fucking thing you have." He tugged Shiloh's belt open roughly.

"It's yours. Fuck, babe. Don't stop." Shiloh shoved his jeans down past his ass, easy as you please, hands wrapping around his cheeks.

All he wanted to do was rut and pant and kiss and shoot all over Shiloh. He pushed his hands into Shiloh's open fly and pressed his hand against that sweet, hard cock, then worked it free until he could get his hand around the shaft.

Shiloh bucked, grunting at his touch. It was a rough, hungry little sound that turned him right on.

He lined up and squeezed their cocks together. "We're gonna do this right here?"

"The momma dog don't care. She's busy." Shiloh's words made him chuckle.

"Right." God, he could hardly breathe. He worked their shafts in one hand and palmed the heads with the other, not caring if this took two minutes or twenty. He needed to feel *more*. A lot more. He couldn't stop his hips from rocking into Shiloh either, and he wasn't the least bit worried about that.

"Mmhmm." Shiloh grabbed his bottom lip with his teeth and tugged. "More."

That little pinch went right to his balls, and Tate groaned. "Yeah." He went harder, letting Shiloh hold him up, ready to give the cowboy anything he asked for.

They grunted and rocked, driving against each other like fiends. Shiloh was right with him, moving with a pure, hungry need.

It was hot as hell, the two of them just getting off together. He could hardly breathe, and his cock jerked against Shiloh's fighting his grip. "Gonna...make a...mess in a minute." Quick and dirty had never felt this good. He swept his thumb across the top of Shiloh's cock the way he knew Shiloh liked.

"Fuck!" The single word snapped out, Shiloh's head popping up as spunk sprayed over his fingers.

And that was more than enough. Tate bucked wildly against Shiloh for a second, then followed his cowboy right off the cliff, gasping and trembling.

Shiloh rested their foreheads together, both of them breathing hard. "Wow. I like the night before a snow day."

"Snow days are sexy." He huffed and took a light kiss, head still swimming. "I like coming home to you."

"I like it too. I mean...this is—good."

"It's so good." He nipped at Shiloh's chin, sticky fingers pressing into that hard belly. "You're really...amazing." That was as eloquent as his hormone-addled brain would allow.

Shiloh nodded, holding him for a minute before cleaning them up, the touch gentle. He watched Shiloh's hands move over him so carefully, it was so sweet the little ways that his cowboy let him know how much he mattered.

"Good enough for puppies, right? We can get a shower later maybe. I'm looking forward to that stew." And the garlic knots—he could eat a dozen of those without thinking twice about it.

"It turned out good. You'll like it." Shiloh dropped a kiss on his jaw. "I'm going to peek in at Annabelle, make sure she's good."

"Okay. I'll stoke up the fire, and then we can eat." He followed Shiloh out of the kitchen and turned the other way to go add a log or two to the fire. They'd be nice and toasty in the living room tonight watching a movie or something.

He headed back to the kitchen and put the rolls back in the oven to warm up a little, then pulled down a bottle of wine. It seemed like a wine kind of night.

"We have three more! That's eight!" Shiloh's eyes were wide, pulling at the edges.

"Eight puppies? Are they all okay? Is she done now? Wait, I need to see. Watch the knots, they're in the oven. I won't go, I just...eight?" Eight puppies. Wow. He hurried to the laundry room.

Sure enough, there were eight tiny black and white bundles of fur, nursing hard while the momma dog rested. "Hey, momma. Are you all done? You look pretty tired. You've got some cute babies though."

She huffed at him and nodded. "I'll let you sleep. Good job, momma." He closed the door slightly and went back to the kitchen. Shiloh had opened the wine and was pouring it. "Wow. Eight."

"Yeah. I sent pics to the vet, so she can come out if she thinks she needs to, but they're all eating."

"I saw that. She might as well have rolled her eyes at me. They're awfully cute though. Tiny." He picked up his glass. "To snow days and kitchen sex. And puppies."

"Hell, yes. Snow, sex, and little fluff balls. I'm in."

"Feed me, baby. I'm hungry." He pulled the garlic knots out of the oven. They smelled like heaven. The kitchen smelled a little like sex and a little like garlic knots.

There was no bad there.

19

"Annabelle, go out and go potty. The puppies are okay."

Messy.

Loud.

Expensive.

Hungry.

Stinky.

But okay.

He and Tate had shoveled a loop around the house and a path to the barn, but it was still snowing, so he could understand that she didn't want to go out.

She stared at him like he had betrayed her in every way, but she tromped out, making him snort.

"Go."

Tate stood in the doorway, arms full. "I've got clean blankets. I had a bunch of old ones in the basement. You want to do a quick change while she's out?"

"Oh, I knew there was a reason I loved you." The words left his mouth before he thought, and once they were out, they were.

"Just the one, huh?" Tate grinned at him, teasing.

His cheeks were burning, but he managed to wink.

"I love you too, you big dope." Tate set the blankets down, gave him a kiss that should have lasted longer, then started sorting puppies into a box so they could clean up.

"Yeah." And it was amazing and wild and unexpected and a little guilt making. Shiloh had believed he had found his one and only for all time, and...now he was in love again. "Thank god for that. It sucks to be in it alone."

"Yeah, but don't worry, baby. I knew. I know." Tate started hauling up dirty towels and blankets and tossing them in the washer.

"Man, do we have any of that extra no-stink stuff? These guys are odiferous." Look at him, pulling out a ten-dollar word.

"If you can write that on the chalkboard and spell it correctly, you get extra credit. Fabric softener." Tate added some to the washer.

"Do I have to use it in a sentence, teach?" he teased and started the washer.

"You just did, didn't you?" Tate shook his head. "Annabelle's in the mudroom. You want to go dry her off? I'm not sure she trusts me yet."

"Sure. She'll get around to liking you, I know it." He grabbed a towel and went to dry off Miss Annabelle.

"I know, I'll try to make friends when she's had some time to rest." Tate called after him. "I'll get the clean stuff down quick."

"You rock. Thank you." He got Annabelle dried up and fed while the pups were sleeping. All the puppies had made it through that first night, and Momma was eating good.

"Okay, she's all set. The pups are out cold in that box too." Tate wandered into the living room and peered out the window. "It's really coming down. Still. I don't know if Nate will make it up tomorrow morning either. I might need more help with the beasts. We'll see."

"You know I will. I don't mind one bit." In fact, he sort of liked the process of milking. It was new and interesting, and he liked being useful. "The greenhouse is holding on like a dream."

"If you're concerned about it, we can get out there with the roof rake tomorrow. Snow can make good insulation, but it can also get heavy as it melts. Hey, girl. You want to go back to your babies?" Tate moved out of their way. He didn't seem afraid of dogs; it looked more like he was taking his time with the new mom.

Annabelle gave Tate the side eye and went to settle, tail thumping.

"Good girl. Okay, what do we need to do? Classwork? Farmwork? Watch a movie? Bake cookies?" He was up for anything.

"Ooh. Cookies. Let's do that." Tate's eyes were wide like a kid's. "I have a stack of papers to grade, and I should check my school email, both of which I could totally do while eating cookies and watching a movie."

"What kind of cookies? Chocolate chip? Peanut butter?" He was easy. "Oatmeal scotchies?"

"Unless you stocked my kitchen when I wasn't looking, I think I have peanut butter...and I might have chocolate chips, but I don't know how long they've been in there." Tate shrugged.

"I'll explore." He had been grocery shopping, so he knew a lot of what was in the kitchen—for example, he knew that he had a dozen different kind of baking chips in a tote, because Christmas was coming, and teachers needed to provide snacks for things. Also, he'd already been tapped for four different bake sales for football, cheerleading, chess club, and student council.

"I can definitely pour coffee." Tate chuckled. "You tell me how I can help."

"No worries. I'll start with pulling out a stick of butter. Somehow that seems to be the basis of most cookies. A stick of butter."

Tate leaned on the counter, curious eyes watching him. "Butter, flour, sugar, chips, vanilla maybe? That's what I remember my mom doing."

"Leavening. You have to have baking powder or soda or both." He dug out the chocolate chip bag, knowing there was a recipe on the back.

"Baking powder...never would have known. You know I'm procrastinating, right? I really don't want to grade papers."

"You can make coffee and admire my cookie-making prowess, then." Shiloh was going to have to nuke the butter a little; it was chilly in here.

"I can. I will. I'm a fan of your...prowess." Tate winked at him.

"I know—I'm the...prowessesseyist." Oh, that was a good one.

"You're an idiot." Tate snorted. "But an amusing one. Did your mother teach you to bake?"

"My granny. She was a sweetheart, and she could bake like a dream." He smiled, because he could remember her like he'd seen her yesterday. She'd smelled like cinnamon and sugar, like anise and vanilla.

"Did she raise you? I know about the ranch you sold, but I don't think you've told me about where you grew up." The coffee started brewing, filling the kitchen with a warm scent.

"She and I were close. I was a latchkey kid—I had a

single mom who worked at a car dealership, doing payroll. She and I had a falling out when I got married." It had been awful and weird, and he'd been crazy in love and willing to do anything for Matt.

"Oh, I'm sorry. Have you seen her at all since?" Tate's fingers slid across his back, the touch reassuring.

"No. No, she and I were evil to each other, and I'm not sure that we can come back from that." He'd been a disappointment to her, and she had said some cutting things that had broken his heart.

If she said, "I told you so" now, he might explode.

"That sounds hard. I'm sorry." Tate leaned on the counter, eyes studying him, fingers playing up and down his arm. "Well, we're parentless then. But we have each other."

"We do. We have each other, we have puppies, we have a greenhouse and cows." He waited a heartbeat, then drawled. "Moo."

That made Tate giggle like a four-year-old. "Moohoo." Tate hugged him from behind, resting his head between his shoulder blades. "I love how many times you just said 'we'. Love it. This farm should be shared."

"It's a great place. It deserves to be adored."

"I was talking more about us, you goon. But yes. That too." Tate peered around him. "Don't you think you should add more chips?"

"You think?" He dumped in more and stirred, nodding. That looked more...decadent.

"Mhm. Doesn't that look better?" Tate took a pinch of dough with his fingers and popped it in his mouth. "Mm!"

"Do we need nuts? Or are you a no-nut nut?"

"Nuts are good. We have nuts? Don't—" Tate cracked up. "Not the sexy kind."

Shiloh had never laughed so much in his life, and he

grabbed Tate up and took a kiss, thanking him the best way he knew how.

Tate hugged him back, grinning into the kiss. "Do I taste like chocolate chips?"

"You do, I think. Let me verify." He stole another kiss. "Mmm...yup. I approve."

Tate's grin never faded, and Shiloh realized he could make Tate happy. He was making the man happy now. "Put me down, brute. Those need to get into the oven so I can eat them."

"Bossy bossy." He kissed the tip of Tate's nose. "I'm on it."

Cookies he could do. And then he had eight minutes in between batches of goodies.

"That's right, minion." Tate poured them mugs of coffee and took them to the living room. "Gonna stoke up the fire and check the snow."

"Make sure it's still there?" he teased. "Give it a firm talking to?"

"Can't be too careful," Tate sang. "We're going to have to redo the dog run by morning. I wonder if they'll cancel school again tomorrow?"

"Then it's a four-day weekend!" He loved that idea. They could be happy shut-ins.

"If I get my grading done we could go skiing tomorrow. Are those cookies in yet? Get out here and look at this."

"Yes, and yes, and okay, coming!"

Tate snorted, "You're not even breathing hard." He pulled Shiloh to the window. "Look. You can't even see Annabelle's tracks anymore. That was fast. It's blowing around too. Wow."

"Lord have mercy." He'd never seen anything like this before. "That's insane."

"It's a lot, but don't worry. I have a generator that powers a system that keeps the pipes warm and the fridge running if we lose power, and a solar battery for phones and plug-in appliances. There's a ton of wood in the shed on the back porch for the wood stove and the fireplace. We'll be fine for a couple of days." He plopped on the couch and dragged his school bag over. "You'll be a Vermonter in no time."

"I believe you." Except he was going to have to ask Sky about that. Somehow he wondered.

Tate was sitting in his favorite grading spot. Shiloh watched as he pulled the lap desk out from next to the couch and set his papers on it, then pulled out a red pen. His lover was so old school. Tate glanced at him. "What?"

"Nothing."

"I like technology, but I like paper more."

Shiloh nodded. There wasn't a single thing wrong with that. "I hear you. There's something about the scratch of pen on paper that you can't beat."

"Well, and math... I feel like you have to work it out on paper, you know? To get it into your brain."

"Yeah?" He was a math and science person himself, really. It was how his brain worked.

"Yeah...you want to see what I mean?" Tate handed him a pen.

"Sure. I'm in." And the cookies would save him if he made an idiot out of himself.

20

W hy the hell did they bother to have school the three days before Thanksgiving? What was the point? With a short Wednesday and a four-day weekend coming, Tate couldn't get anything done. It wasn't quite as bad as the week before Christmas break, but it was close.

Maybe he should have planned a test or something to keep the kids' heads in the game a little. But that just seemed mean, and he didn't like to set his students up to fail.

So instead, he was driving home from school hungry and with a pounding headache, papers to grade, and a day and a half to survive before it was all over. Maybe Shiloh had cooked. Not that it was his job, but he often did, and he was good at it.

He pulled into the driveway, which he'd finally had plowed so they could maneuver both of their trucks without having to pull into the street. He'd known the plow guy a while; he was the father of one of the teachers at school—a retiree who loved to have something to do. He'd plowed the whole property, including out back so Shiloh could get to and from the greenhouse.

He groaned as he got out of the truck. He needed Tylenol and maybe a cup of coffee. Maybe he'd put the homework papers off until tomorrow and just put his feet up by the fire for a while.

He heard the ruckus before the door closed.

Bark!

Bark bark! Grr. Rawr. Yip yip.

Then, "Y'all crack me up!"

Oh god. Puppies. So many puppies. They were cute, but they weren't quiet. He tugged off his boots and went straight to the kitchen where he pulled a bottle of Tylenol from his junk drawer.

The house smelled like wet dog, the whole laundry room was taken over, and—well, okay, there was obviously something that smelled good in the oven. Lasagna, maybe? He swallowed the Tylenol with a fistful of water from the kitchen sink and then peered into the oven. Yeah. Lasagna. And there were some yummy-looking rolls on the counter too.

He took a deep breath and headed for the laundry room, following Shiloh's happy laughter. It was hard to be grumpy listening to that laugh, and he found a smile by the time he reached the door. "Someone is having fun in here."

"Come see, babe. They're trying to get out of the whelping box, and Bubbles is trying to convince her sibs to create a ladder. Goose is having none of that nonsense."

All eight puppies had names. *Names.*

He peered into the box. They were really cute, he had to admit. But that didn't mean he wanted eight dogs on the farm. Nine, actually, counting Mama. Poor Annabelle looked as exhausted as he felt. She'd really taken to him over the last few days, though. When she needed a break from the pups she'd track him down for belly rubs and treats and flop on the couch with him for a minute.

"Dinner smells really good." That was nice to say right? He tried to keep the headache and the holiday week stress out of his voice.

"Lasagna. I thought you could take some to work tomorrow. You looking forward to Thanksgiving?"

He sighed. "I'm trying. Mostly, I'm looking forward to this week being over."

"Oh, honey. I'm sorry. What can I do? You ask, I'll make it happen."

Give the puppies some Benadryl so they'll sleep? Obviously he wasn't going to ask that. "I just have a headache. The kids are so punchy, they're half on vacation already. I took some Tylenol, and I think dinner will help."

"Well, go have a sit on the sofa. I'm going to make sure everything is settled for the night in here, and then I'll get to finishing supper and all."

"Hey, girl." He reached in and gave Annabelle a little love. "Too bad it's not warmer; we could put all the puppies in the barn."

"They'd love that, huh? They're too little, but...well, by spring, they'll be able to leave Annabelle. I'm assuming you don't want to keep them all?"

"Do we need to keep any?" That popped right out, and he instantly regretted it.

There was a long silence, but when he looked over, Shiloh was moving into the kitchen. "Don't forget to close the laundry room door, so they'll sleep, please."

"Oh, Annabelle. I'm in trouble. You get some rest, Mama." He closed the door quietly and followed Shiloh to the kitchen. "I said it, but it's not really what I meant. My head is killing me."

"No worries. You go sit and close your eyes. The lasagna will be ready at five thirty, give or take."

"Okay. Thank you." He nodded and did exactly that. He had questions and more to say, but he obviously wasn't worth anything with his head pounding, so he decided the conversation should wait. He stretched out on the couch, which he'd been very familiar with sleeping all night on before Shiloh made him want to sleep in a bed again, so he dozed off as soon as he closed his eyes.

When he woke up, it was eight o'clock, black as pitch, and he found Shiloh in the overstuffed chair, earphones in, reading on his phone.

He sat up slowly, blinking to focus. "It's past five thirty, isn't it?"

It took Shiloh a second to hear him, then he got a grin and a nod. "The lasagna will warm up like a dream."

He shuffled over to the chair and perched in Shiloh's lap feeling like he needed to make it up to the cowboy. "Sorry I fell asleep. Did you eat?"

"I didn't. I figured I could wait until you woke up."

"My headache seems to be gone." He rubbed his forehead, like that would help him make sure. "I'm sorry for...being short-tempered."

"No worries. I'm glad you're feeling better." There was a little subdued tone in Shiloh's voice, but nothing strong enough to comment on.

"Can we eat? Are you hungry?" He combed his fingers through Shiloh's hair. He knew what was up. He'd slammed the door on the puppy thing. He was going to have to reopen that conversation, but...food first.

"Sure. Hop up. The salad's all made. I just have to heat

the casserole and the bread." Shiloh patted his butt, encouraging him to stand.

He wiggled against Shiloh's hand before he got up. "You made a salad too? You're too good to me." Way too good for the grumpy teacher that came home a couple of hours ago.

"Yeah, I harvested some from the greenhouse today, plus there were some good cherry tomatoes at the store."

"Salad from your greenhouse? How cool!" He followed Shiloh into the kitchen. "It's going to be the most delicious salad ever."

"Yeah. It's growing well, and it's got good flavor." Shiloh started the oven, and then pulled out a bowl of salad from the fridge. "I didn't dress it. What do you want?"

"Is there more of that red wine vinaigrette you made?" Tate poked at the salad. "Are you excited to be harvesting?"

"Yes, and yeah, it's an interesting experiment, and I'm glad it's working. I'm tickled that you let me try it out."

"You love it. I'm so excited to make this place more than I could by myself."

Shiloh shot him a wink. "I'm getting it set up."

"You certainly have in the kitchen. And possibly the bedroom." Tate grabbed his hand and kissed it. He was going to jolly Shiloh out of this heavy stillness.

"Only possibly, huh?" One eyebrow lifted, but that got him a grin.

"Well, you know how it is. Two sides to every story? Considering I bought the bed when I moved in, put a set of sheets on it and then never slept in it, I'd say you improved it."

"I'll take it. I hope so. I want to."

"You know I'm joking, right? Is this really a question? You improved a lot more than the house just by sitting in the corner of the bar and looking like someone I wanted to talk to."

Shiloh chuckled and shook his head. "I bet they miss me. I like the new joint I'm hanging out at, way more…"

"Right? My couch is way more comfy. I bet that booth has your butt indented in it."

"I have zero doubt. It probably still smells like me." Shiloh managed to say that with a straight face, which Tate thought was impressive as hell.

"There are worse things." He peered at the lasagna warming in the oven. If he didn't look at Shiloh he might be able to keep a straight face too. "Cow patties, skunk, dog farts."

"Don't forget rotten eggs. Those can be intense."

Oh, sulfur was something every teacher understood.

"Ooh." He chuckled. "Way worse." He slid his arms around Shiloh's waist. "The lasagna smells amazing though."

"Yeah, it's a lot of work, but I love how we can nosh on it for a couple of days." Shiloh leaned toward him, letting him feel some weight.

Tate hugged him harder. "I'm not avoiding. We should talk, I know. You want to have dinner and then we can settle in by the fire?"

"Sure. I'm not stressed."

No, in fact Shiloh seemed Zen.

It was a little disconcerting. What was he so Zen about? It was like he knew something Tate didn't. He let Shiloh go and put a trivet out on the counter for the lasagna. "Cool. Ready to eat?"

"Yes, I'm starving, man. I mean, I'm empty as a worm." The bread and salad landed on the table.

"Thank you for waiting for me." He pulled the hot pan

out of the oven. It looked incredible. "You are such a good cook."

"I like it." Shiloh stood there, seeming uncomfortable for a minute, like he wasn't sure what to do. "What do you want to drink?"

"Just water for me. Thanks. What do you serve this with? A spatula? A big spoon?"

"A spatula, I think. The best parts are the bits at the bottom, right?"

"I haven't had lasagna in so long I forgot that." He pulled out a spatula and dug in, serving up two plates as his stomach growled. "Ooh. I'm hungry. A few bites of this and I'll be a real human again."

"As opposed to?" Shiloh chuckled, and Tate could hear Shiloh's stomach answering his. "God, it does smell like heaven. I may have seconds."

"As opposed to the cranky monster that walked in after school today." He shrugged apologetically.

"It was a hard day, huh? I'm sorry." Shiloh shook his head. "It was pretty peaceful here."

He wasn't sure he'd call a pile of puppies peaceful, but Shiloh obviously felt differently about them than he did. He was going to have to work on that. "The kids are just ready to be on skis and not in the classroom. It's hard to get anything done, and even if I don't plan much, I still have to keep them occupied, you know?"

"I can only imagine. I remember being in school Thanksgiving week and just waiting for that Tuesday afternoon bell to ring."

"Yes. And here it's Wednesday lunchtime, even worse. I get it, but I kind of wish they'd just close the whole week. Maybe I'll take preventative Advil tomorrow." He took a bite of his lasagna, and the tangy sauce and warm cheese were comforting. "Mmm. Baby, this is so good."

"I'll send you some for lunch tomorrow, huh?" Shiloh tucked in, humming softly under his breath.

"That will definitely make my day better," he said with his mouth full.

Shiloh bobbed his head, licking tomato sauce off his bottom lip. "Excellent. I do like this."

"You're hungry. Thank you for waiting for me; you didn't have to do that." But he would have done it for Shiloh too, and one of the reasons he knew pretty deep down that this was the real thing.

That, and the lasagna tasted like love.

The kitchen went quiet while they both ate like this was their last meal on earth.

S hiloh headed to the greenhouse, deep in thought.

In worry, really.

Somehow, he had fallen into the same basic spot he'd been in with Matty. Well-loved, well-kept, but he was basically taking care of the plants, the house, the cooking, and dogs that Tate didn't even want.

He was playing house in someone else's home.

He opened the door to the greenhouse and closed it behind him, letting the warmth and the smell of growing surround him. He needed a plan.

"What would you do, Matty?" He sort of knew the answer. Matt would have gone to rodeo, thrown himself on one bull after another until he didn't have to think or feel anything anymore. "Okay, what would you tell me to do?"

He got no answer, which seemed incredibly unfair, but his phone did ring, Sky's name popping up. He put the phone on speaker and got to work. "Hey, cowboy."

"Howdy. How goes?" It was like Sky had radar.

"I think I've fucked up." Again.

"Uh-oh. Let me get another cup of coffee. You want to come over? I'll make another pot."

He checked the hydration on another pot, nodding like Sky could hear him. "Do you mind?"

"Nope. I'm hanging out with Sierra. Noah and Charlie are at school."

Praise Jesus. "I'll be there in thirty."

He made it in twenty, some leftover coffee cake in hand.

"Sierra just went down for a nap, sorry you missed her."

"Maybe I'll check on her before I leave."

"Good idea." Sky glanced at his coffee cake. "It's like you know I'm a much better listener when I've been fed." Sky pushed a mug in his direction and picked up his own.

"It's a thing." He grabbed two forks. They didn't stand on ceremony.

Sky waited for him to sit before poking. "Did you cheat on him?"

"What? No! Never!" Like he'd do that. "Sky!"

"Well, that's the big one. Everything else is forgivable." Sky's grin was evil as fuck. "So spill."

"So, you know about the puppies—" Shiloh started talking. About the dogs, the house, the greenhouse, and the sinking suspicion that he was living someone else's life, again. "It wasn't even that Tate isn't interested in having dogs, but the first thing I thought was, 'this is his house,' and it's true. I'm staying in his house. It's like it was with Matt. I was living at the ranch, growing plants and...what? I mean, I'm just a support person to someone else's life again."

"And what did he say when you told him that?" Sky looked completely serious.

"Told him what?" Like he was going to tell Tate that he was an asshole. "I don't even know what to say yet. That's why I'm here, man."

"Okay." Sky sipped his coffee looking pensive. "Well, how serious are things now? Are you playing house or is this real? Would you stay if things got better? Do you love him?"

"I do, and I'm not leaving him. That's not on the table. I —He's not like Matty, you know, but I'm not the same either. I was a kid, and Matt and I were living like our asses were on fire." Shiloh sighed because it was different now, it was easier, slower, but deeper. This was a steady ember with flames, not a lit fuse that was leading to dynamite. "Maybe I just need to get a job."

Sky snorted. "You have a job. You live on a farm. You need to feel like you own it, Shi. That's what was wrong with Matty, as much as you loved him. He thought of it as his place even with you there."

"Okay, so how did you do it? You came here. How did you feel like you owned it?" It was a fair question, he thought.

"Dude, I'm a bull rider. I own the entire goddamn world."

"Yeah, yeah—"

"I'm serious. You're a Texan. You have a damn fruit and vegetable degree. You got money; I know you do. Go take some ownership, lift your chin, and talk to the son of the bitch that you love."

He crossed his arms and leaned back in his seat. He knew he was scowling. That all sounded too damn easy, which is what made it seem so hard. "I don't know."

"What are you afraid of?"

"Losing everything again." That was easy. He'd survived hell once. "And being lost."

"I don't know Tate well, but I don't think he's going to let you go just because you want your house to feel like yours. Or because you're attached to some puppies."

"Yeah." He was going to get new homes for all of them, as soon as they were old enough. "I just miss my dog. This isn't like Texas, you know? This isn't a ranch, and Tate doesn't need a pack." He sighed and stood. "I'm going to go. I'm building up a sick headache, man." And tomorrow was Thanksgiving. Fuck. "Thanks for the chat."

But this was something he was going to have to figure out on his own.

"Whoa. Hey." Sky stood with him. "If you don't speak up, you can't expect him to understand. That's on you. Talk to him. Tell him what you need."

"I will." Once he figured that out. "I'm not trying to create drama. I'm trying to avoid it."

"I know. But think about whether you should." Sky, patted his shoulder. "And don't be late for Thanksgiving dinner. Charlie's a lot less grumpy about her leg, but she still might not forgive you."

"I won't be. I've got the pies ready to go in the oven, and the French onion dip is made up."

"Good deal. You know I like pie." Sky followed him out. "I don't feel like I was much help. I'm sorry."

"Dude, I needed a friend. You weren't supposed to fix it, just listen to me bitch about it and go, 'yeah, motherfucker'."

Sky laughed. "Over coffee cake. Am I old, or are you?"

"We both are, man. You. Me. We're friggin' ancient." He had to laugh. Had to.

"Okay, then. We'll sit and eat coffee cake, I'll give you an Excedrin, and we'll talk food and football like real men, fair?"

"Now you're talking, buddy."

Sky grinned at him, winked. "Yeah, motherfucker."

He headed for his truck, smiling for the moment. "Call

me if you need us to pick anything up last minute on our way over. We'll see you tomorrow."

"We'll be here with bells on. Have a good one." He was going to get home about the same time as Tate, if he was lucky.

It was snowing again by the time he got home. Not hard, but enough that Tate's truck left tracks in the driveway, and there was a fresh dusting on the front porch.

He went in through the back door, letting Annabelle out and cleaning up the newspaper from the puppies.

"Hey, there!" Tate called from the living room. "I was going to do that, I just wanted to get the wood stove fired up. It was getting chilly in here."

"Hey. Sorry. I was out and about. How are we doing on wood?" How are we doing?

"Um... I guess we should haul some more in before it gets dark. Let me grab some gloves. Were you doing something fun?" Tate ducked into the mudroom and came back with two sets of gloves.

"Went to have a cup of coffee with Sky." He took one set. "Thanks. How was your day?"

"It was...short." Tate chuckled and leaned in for a kiss. "I'm glad to be on break."

He gave it, and it helped, more than a little. It felt like heaven, in fact.

"Mmm. I needed that. You're totally entitled to your own life, but I missed coming home to you today. I guess that's good. I should miss you once in a while so I remember how much I like having you here."

Oh. That made him smile, and it eased his headache a bit. "Thank you, love."

"Thank you." Tate pulled on his gloves and held the

back door for him. "We should just do a light dinner tonight, huh? With tomorrow being a big food day?"

"There's leftover lasagna, but we could just have a hot turkey sandwich and a salad?" Easy worked for him. He wanted something simple.

"Turkey is for tomorrow. Let's have the lasagna; it was so good. We can just skip the rolls." Tate loaded him up with wood and grabbed a bunch himself.

"That works. Or we can have bacon and eggs." Breakfast for supper was always a win.

"I should really keep chickens, huh? It can't be that hard." They loaded up the rack by the wood stove. "Do you know about chickens?" Annabelle followed them in, and Tate toweled her off before letting her go back to her pups.

"You should, and Matty had them on the ranch, so yes, I do, but I've never kept them where it's cold."

"Hm. We'll have to research. Seems like something the farm needs." Tate looked thoughtful. "Annabelle can herd them around."

He didn't know what to say about that, so he shrugged, feeling unsure and uncomfortable and weird. "That's up to you, honey."

Tate's look said exactly that. Uncomfortable and weird. "...okay." Tate shook his head and headed for the kitchen. "You want a drink? Are you hungry yet?"

"I'm not hungry, no. In fact, I'm a little queasy," he admitted.

That stopped Tate in his tracks, and he turned around and came right back. "What's the matter? All of a sudden? Do you want to sit down?" Tate looked genuinely worried, like he was about to have a heart attack or something.

"I'm a little acidy, I think. I just want to be with you for a little while, yeah?" He just wanted to figure things out.

That didn't make Tate look any less worried. "Yeah, okay. Give me your gloves. We'll just sit and enjoy the fire, and... be warm."

"Yeah. I think that sounds like heaven. Seriously. I've—" He what? Needed to talk? Fuck. He stood there awkwardly while Tate put their gloves away.

"Are you tired? Come lie on me, baby." Tate sat and patted his thigh. "Get comfy."

Feeling a little silly, he took the offer and leaned down, resting his cheek on Tate's leg. "You're warm."

"Mhm. I got toasty making the fire." Tate stroked fingers through his hair.

He didn't fall asleep, but he let himself relax and doze, be heavy against Tate's leg.

They sat there for a few minutes, just quietly, listening to the fire until Annabelle appeared with a puppy in her mouth and set it on the couch behind Shiloh's knees.

"Hey...oh. Wow." Tate sounded surprised when she returned with another. "We have visitors."

"What's the matter, little momma? You worried you're not safe in there alone?"

She wagged, then disappeared before bringing another pup.

The pups climbed around on the couch, sitting on him and on Tate until she had them all accounted for. She checked them all over, then went and curled up by the fire and let out a long sigh.

Tate was giggling, playing with puppies. "I guess she figured we could babysit since we're sitting here anyway?"

"I guess so." He shook his head. "These guys are so damn cute."

"They're so funny. Which one is this?" Tate pointed to a puppy that had curled up behind his shoulder.

"That's little Bean. He's the runt, and he's a snugglebug."

"He's so sweet. What's that one's name?" Tate pointed to the black and white pup chewing on his belt.

"Clara Bow. She's fierce and squeaky."

"That's a cute name. And who's the black one?" Tate reached out to give the pup a scritch.

"Ray-Ray." He sighed, and just said what was on his mind. "I know we can't keep them, but I had to name them."

"I shouldn't have said that." Tate said quickly, like it had been on the tip of his tongue. "I was in a foul mood; I had a headache and you all were making noise and I just... I'm sorry. What do you think about keeping these three?"

"What about Annabelle? Because she's special." And he'd love to have the four, but Annabelle had proved herself to be a good dog.

"Oh. We have to keep her. Of course. We're finally starting to be friends." Tate sighed. "She likes it here."

"So do I." Come on, Shiloh. You're in a good place. "I want—I need to be... I mean, fuck, I want this to be home too, you know? Does that make sense?"

"It is—" Tate stopped himself. "Sorry. You don't feel like it's home, you mean?"

"I mean, I feel like it's yours, and I want it to be ours. I want us to be...a partnership."

"I want that too. I thought I was trying to make you feel that way, but—I mean the greenhouse is yours and we share a bed... I haven't paid for groceries since you moved in. But...what do you need?"

"I don't know. Maybe I need to contribute more? I mean...what if I match what you make from the milk deliveries? That way you're not working so hard."

"Yeah? That would be cool, then I wouldn't need the second job. More time to learn the cheese thing." Tate caught a pup that was headed for the edge of the couch. "We also could use that money to hire someone to help you clear some land in the spring and plant whatever you think we can grow. I don't work in the summer much; we could do farmers markets, maybe? Could be fun."

"I'd love that." More than anything, he loved the easy acceptance. How Tate was with him. "We're going to have tomatoes soon, and cukes too. Fresh in the middle of winter."

"That's wild. I love cucumbers with a tiny bit of salt and some paprika. Yum."

"Paprika, huh? I'd try that."

All the puppies were sound asleep, the sun was almost gone, and the fire was perfect. He inhaled deep and then let it all out.

"I'd love to keep the three puppies and Annabelle, and I want to cover so that you only have to teach and have the farm."

Money wasn't his problem. Matty had made sure of that.

"Okay. And I want you to break the lease on that apartment finally." When he turned his head, Tate shrugged. "I know you've been hanging onto it, but I didn't know why. If you want this to be your home, then move in with both feet."

"I'll call Monday and take care of it. It's empty anyway. I have one of those portable storage buildings with some personal things. I'd like to bring them here."

"Yes, please. I'm not really attached to any furniture in the house, so we can move stuff out to make room for the things you care about. I'd like that. I'd like to have more of you around here."

"I would too. I—You know, I moved into Matty's ranch,

and I felt like I was a visitor sometimes. Not always, but sometimes." And sometimes it liked to break his heart.

"Oh, Shi." Tate's fingers slipped down under his chin. "I don't want you to feel that way. You're half my heart now; you should feel like this is half your house. I'm glad you said something."

"I didn't know what to say, but I'm tickled you heard me." Because that was solid.

"I'm used to listening to teenagers. I'm pretty good at deciphering." Tate chuckled. "What are we going to do with the other pups? Do you want me to put up a flyer at school? And I guess we should get Annabelle spayed; I don't think she'll want to do this again." Annabelle was sound asleep by the fire.

"We should definitely get her fixed, and yeah, if you know good people. I'm thinking Sky and Beck might be getting ready for another pup, and they might know people too." He wanted them all to have good homes.

"Maybe you could give one to Charlie for Christmas."

"Maybe, if her dads are into it, yeah. I'll ask." That was a great idea. So he told that to his lover.

Tate bent and kissed him upside down, smiling as he pulled away. "I'm going to be very thankful tomorrow. And I don't mean about the turkey."

"No?" he teased. "About the pies?"

"With ice cream. How did you guess?" Tate tickled him under his armpit.

"I'm a smart, smart son of a bitch." Thankful too.

Good thing it was the time of year for it.

22

"Papa! Pappy, football!" Charlie waved from the couch where she was sitting with Bruiser who was not so subtly begging for her pretzels.

Tate shook his head. He knew Thanksgiving was a big football day, and usually that was how he spent it—eating turkey sandwiches and watching football—but he realized suddenly that he didn't even know who was playing. He was so excited about spending the day with Shiloh, and the people Shiloh considered family that he'd completely forgotten all about football.

"Pap! Fooba!" Okay. That was cute. Almost as cute as Sierra's tiny Dallas Cowboys Cheerleaders outfit and itty-bitty pompoms.

"I hear you! I was helping Papa check on the turkey."

"He's gonna miss the kickoff." Charlie shook her head like she was disappointed in Sky, and he covered his grin.

"She really likes her football, huh?" He leaned back against Shiloh who was watching all this unfold with him.

"She really does. Her grampa loves football too, and—"

"Papa! Grampy! Y'all come on! You promised! Pappy can make the dam-durned sausage balls with Granny!"

Shiloh's eyes went wide, and he bit his bottom lip.

"Young lady." Beckett's father strolled out of the kitchen, giving her a disapproving look.

"Sorry. Sorry but..." she pointed. "It's gonna start!"

"I'm going to see if I can help," he gave Shiloh a wink and headed into the kitchen, where Sky and his mom were busy. Noah sat at the kitchen table, looking at a book. "Oh, man. It smells good in here."

"Yes, and I'm about to have a hysterical baby girl if I don't get in there and cheer." Sky winked over at him. "Can you keep an eye on Noah for me until Beck reappears, please?"

"I totally can. Go on, go...."

Sky nodded his thanks and Tate got out of his way as he hurried out of the kitchen. "Hi." He gave Beck's mom a wave. "I'm Tate."

"Hello, Tate. I'm Laura. You're a friend of Shiloh's?"

"More than a friend, but yes. I came with Shiloh."

"Oh, good for him." Laura rolled her eyes. "And for you, of course, but Sky worries about him."

"He's a widower, but well, he's living with—" No. No, that wasn't right. "We've moved in together."

Laura winked at him. "It's new, huh? Don't worry. It gets easier to talk about. Words matter."

"Right? They really do. I'm..." He was an only child, and he'd lived alone his whole life. Sharing was...new. "Learning."

Laura pushed a dish in front of him and handed him some cheese. "Grate that, bury the pasta in it and I'll put it in the oven. I cooked it yesterday, but the kids love cheese."

"Shiloh is a really good cook, you know. I should get him in here."

Laura laughed. "It's a cheese grater. You can handle it."

"You never know. We might have grated fingers."

"Cheese!" Noah cheered, making them both laugh.

"All right, all right. Cheese it is." He could certainly grate cheese; he just felt a little self-conscious hanging out with someone's mother. He felt like a teenager again. He started grating, dumping the cheese on top as he went. It was kind of relaxing in a weird way.

Beckett came back through, carrying an armful of wood. "Hey, there. Mom put you to work, did she?"

"She did. She was smart enough not to give me anything too complicated. How was kickoff?"

"Cowboys are having a good year. All's well in my world. Now if they don't win this game? Dinner might be tense." Beck rolled his eyes. "Noah, you want to help me load up the stove?"

Noah put his book down and slid off his chair. "Coming, Pappy!"

What a beautiful, serious little guy.

Warm hands landed on his shoulders, rubbing. "Hey, babe."

"Mm." That felt good. "Hi. I'm grating cheese. I'm almost done."

"Shiloh, have a look at the turkey for me, will you? Sky says it's done but I don't know. Half his mind was on that game."

"Yes, ma'am." Shiloh grabbed the thermometer from the drawer next to the stove and checked. "It's ready to come out. You want me to pull it?"

"Please. Put it up on the stove and cover it."

"We can trade for this, it's all cheesealicious and ready to warm up." He stayed out of Shiloh's way, then tucked the mac & cheese into the oven after the turkey was out. "That looks amazing."

"Smells pretty good too. Did you want me to put the jalapeno popper dip out or wait?" Shiloh's grin threatened to light up the room.

"Oh, I'd forgotten, Shiloh. Why don't you take it out for the folks watching the game?"

"No worries. I'm on it." Shiloh tossed him some tortilla chips. "Come on, honey. Let's feed the fans."

He caught the bag. "You okay here, Laura?"

"I'm fine, honey." She gave him a kind smile. "Football isn't my thing, and Beck will be back in a minute. You go have fun."

"Okay. Just call me if you need more help." He hated leaving her on her own, but Beck was already headed past them as they left the kitchen.

"It's a jungle out there," Beckett warned.

"Good to know."

They headed out, Charlie and Beck's dad yelling at the television, Sierra cheering and waving her pompoms, and Sky watching the game through his eyelids.

They set the food down and for a second, the game was totally forgotten. Even Charlie dug in.

"Are we winning?"

"Of course we are!" Charlie's mouth was full.

"Yay!" Sierra opened her mouth and Beck's dad stuck a chip in with a tiny amount of dip.

He curled an arm around Shiloh. "I think Sky's enjoying the game the most."

"He's got the right idea, doesn't he?" Shiloh leaned back into his arm. "I have jalapeno popper dip. It's Charlie spicy, not Sky spicy."

"Charlie seems to be enjoying it. I'm not sure any of us

are ready for Sky spicy anyway." He watched the kids, wondering if he and Shiloh would be bringing kids to Thanksgiving one day. "You think we could do this?"

"Have a family or host Thanksgiving?" Shiloh teased.

"Sit and watch football. Duh." He rolled his eyes. "Family. No one wants me to host Thanksgiving. Although I guess you could manage it."

"I could, but this is nice. We can host a Christmas party." Shiloh glanced at him. "Dogs need kids. So do farms, so..."

"Oh. Dogs and farms need kids." He poked Shiloh playfully in the side. "But does Shiloh?"

SHILOH SAT in their front room with a finger of whiskey in a glass.

Thanksgiving dinner had been amazing and filling. They had enough leftovers to eat for two days. The puppies had been in and out, and three more puppies had been spoken for. That only left two, and Tate hadn't even talked to his friends at the school.

Life was pretty damn good.

Tate was on the floor with a glass of wine, grading math tests at the coffee table and leaning back against the couch right next to his knees.

"I'm almost done. Man, I have a couple of things I'm going to have to review with these kids. It's not very often I pull questions off the test and call them extra credit. That's on me. Bummer."

"Damn. Well, they'll all figure it out. You're one hell of a teacher." He, on the other hand, just grew shit.

"Sometimes I think so, sometimes I think...why do these people trust me with their children's minds?" Tate chuckled and entered something into a spreadsheet on his laptop before closing it. "Enough for tonight."

"It's a holiday, right? Come snuggle." He found that he wanted to talk, if he was honest. Did Tate want children? How many? How did he want to go about it?

Tate climbed up on the couch, took a sip of his wine, then leaned against him. "It is, you're right. Mm. You're comfortable."

"I am. Did you have a good turkey day?" He wrapped Tate up in one arm.

"I really did. I'm usually on my own, and they're great company. Beck's parents are nice, she's a great cook...it was just really nice. You?"

"It was. I liked sharing the work and the fun with their family. I loved Sierra in that little outfit."

"She's a hoot, right? And Noah is so sweet and gentle."

Shiloh chuckled and nodded. "He had to be, to contrast with Charlie. That little girl is a firecracker."

"She is a force to be reckoned with for sure. They're so good with her though. Did you hear her say she wants to play football?"

"Sky's got her signed up for PeeWee football for the summer. Beck is not amused."

Tate snorted. "I remember Beck saying he wasn't so amused about the barrel racing and the bull riding either. Something tells me there's no stopping her if she's determined."

"Yeah. Sky's already got that little one racing. She rides better than I do."

Tate turned his head to look at him. "We need horses. You could teach me to ride."

"I could. Do you want to start a family with me, do you think?" That was smooth and well-delivered...

Tate blinked at him. "What? I was talking horses...did you just ask me about kids?"

"Yeah. I mean, you've brought it up a couple times..." He knew he hadn't misunderstood. He knew it. Dammit.

"I have." Tate smiled at him. "I usually slide it in a little more gracefully but..."

"Grace isn't my strong suit. I tend to either say what's on my mind or keep my mouth shut, you know?"

"Well then, bluntly, the answer is yes. What's the next question." Tate chuckled against him.

"Did you want to have your biological babies? Or foster babies? Or adopt babies? Or kids?" Oh, that was more than one.

"Yes! All of that." Tate laughed. "We'd need to build an extension on the house though."

"We would." But look at Tate's eyes light up. This wasn't a whim. This was something Tate craved. "There's room for that, though. We could do out or up."

"We should do both. An extension with stairs. I don't think you should foster. You see how that went with the puppies..." Tate was teasing him, but he could tell Tate would have trouble giving a foster child up.

"I do. I get it. I—think that, before we bring children in, I would like to be married. I'm old-fashioned that way. It's important to me—the legal protection, the social appearance." And he wanted things to be right.

"First you ask to move in, then you ask me to marry you, what's next? Kids? Oh wait..." Tate laughed. "I guess if you want to marry me you better come up with a ring."

"Good to know." He would have to search for a good one, and possibly pray on what day to ask. "Either that, or you could ask me."

Tate's eyes lit up again. "I could. I could ask you right now."

Oh. Okay. "It would be only fair, since I asked to move in."

"Okay. Okay, you...stay right here. I'll be right back." Tate kissed his cheek and hopped up, disappearing into the bedroom. "I'll just be a minute."

"All right..." Where on earth was Tate going? It wasn't like the man had a ring waiting on him to ask to be asked.

"Okay. So... I hadn't planned this, but I just thought... well. Let me show you." Tate held out his hand and sitting on his palm was a plain, wide, gold ring. It was clearly a man's ring and looked like a wedding band. "This was my father's."

"Oh." He touched the ring with one fingertip. "It's beautiful."

And special.

And utterly unexpected.

"It's not fancy but it's meaningful to me, and one of the few family things I have. We can save it for our little wedding day, or I can put it on your finger now." Tate slid to one knee. "Either way, Mr. Shiloh Williams, will you marry me?"

He didn't have to think about it, and he didn't worry about the past. He just nodded and said, "Yes. Yes, please."

"Yay!" Tate put the ring on his finger and climbed into his lap. "We can do it here, just a small thing. But, romantic. Maybe more than this proposal." Tate was all smiles and blushing. "Oh my god, we're getting married."

"So long as Beck, Sky and the kids are here, my family will be here." And small and happy sounded perfect.

"Of course! And a couple of my friends, and Nash...that's

enough. We know what we know." Tate kissed him in that sweet, slow way he did when they had nowhere better to be.

We know what we know. He liked that a lot. "Do you want to do it around Christmas? In the spring?"

"Oh, wow. Well...let's not overshadow our first Christmas. Let's do it in the spring—the late spring after mud season so we can do it outside. Unless you don't want to wait that long, then we could do inside."

"Spring is perfect. We'll have pictures, and it'll be amazing, filled with flowers." That suited him.

"When was your other wedding?"

"Halloween in Las Vegas." By Elvis.

Tate laughed. "Fancy. Well you can't say this won't be different."

It did, and that worked. "I think it sounds perfect and very, very us."

"The small and quiet part, or 'hey you wanna get married' part?"

"The intimate, beautiful, filled with family and flowers part." He wasn't going to let Tate make this less than it was.

"Oh, I like that. It sounds much more romantic. I still can't believe it. Thank you for saying yes. You're my person, baby."

"Thank you for asking." He pulled Tate in close. "Kiss me."

"I'll do you one better. Take me to bed." Tate kissed him, not sweet like before, but with a hungry tongue and teeth nipping at his lower nip.

"Oh, I like how you think." Shiloh left the booze behind. He didn't need it for warmth. He had Tate.

He had his fiancé.

23

"All fixed." Tate turned the heater back on and screwed down the top of the waterer. "You know you want a puppy, Nash."

"No. No, I don't want a puppy. That's way too much responsibility. I can't even keep track of my boyfriends."

He shook his head. "You do pretty well with the cows."

"Yeah, well, they're big. It's hard to forget about them. Speaking of boyfriends, where's yours?"

"My *fiancé* is running some errands. He needed something for the greenhouse." He liked how the word rolled off his tongue. He was still kind of stunned, but he was happy something good came out of those big talks.

"Your—dude! Really? A fiancé? You go from no hookups to a hookup to a fiancé?"

"I did! I know. It's nuts, I'm kind of terrified. But it's happening." The ring was a little small for Shiloh, but they'd get it sized before the wedding. "We haven't even told people yet...you might be the first."

"When are you going to do it? Are you going to have the puppies in the wedding?"

He chuckled and punched Nash in the arm. "No, idiot. No puppies. But we're doing it here on the farm, late in the spring after mud season. Don't worry, you'll get an invitation." It might be a text message, but it would be an invitation.

"You'd better. I'll even do the ceremony, if you need it. I am an ordained minister, you know?"

"What? You are?" Nash, a minister? Of what? Weed? "What are you ordained in?"

"I got it off the internet, man. It's like the church of the world and glory or somesuch."

He had to ask, because this was so confusing. And fascinating. "Why?"

"For when friends need to get married." Like that was that. Like there was a calling for it.

"Nash, you are the oddest bird I know. But I have need of an officiant, so you're in!" He gave Nash a quick, spontaneous hug. "It's going to be low key. Assuming I don't freak out before then."

"Eh, Shiloh's not a big stressy guy. He'll be a good husband."

"I know, but will I?" He'd already made Shiloh feel like a guest without realizing it. What if he did that again? What if they didn't agree about something with the house or the land? What if they had kids and they didn't agree on parenting?

He could totally blow this.

"Sure you will. You're a good guy. You two make a good couple—he cooks and grows shit, you teach and make shit. You both learn shit. It's nice."

"That's a lot of shit." He poked Nash, then checked on the water levels for the cows. He didn't think it had been frozen for very long...a few hours maybe. "Looks like everybody is good."

One of the lead cows poked her head in, head bobbing. She was a sweetheart, gentle and easy to love.

"Hey, Daisy." He wandered over and gave her a pat. "The water is all fixed. Is everyone following you? Nash? Are they all headed in?"

"Looks like. Must be about to snow hard."

"They always seem to know. You want to fire up the blower to warm it up in here? Once they're in you should head home so you don't get stuck."

"I'm more worried about Shiloh. He's in town."

"Oh, right. I forgot." He hadn't even thought to worry about Shiloh; Shiloh was so...capable. But now he was. Just a little. "He's got a big truck; he'll be okay," he said, mostly trying to convince himself.

"He'll have to learn. No worries. I'll warm it up in here."

He nodded and got to work, encouraging Daisy to move to the back corner and make room for everyone. By the time he got the doors closed and they wrestled the curtains in place, he was plenty warm, and the cows would be too.

"Don't stress the drive if it's bad in the morning. Shiloh and I can handle this."

"I love this job!" Nash winked at him. "Okay, I'm heading out. Take care of yourself, boss."

Nash chuckled and hopped into his old truck, waving as he left.

"Drive safe," he said to Nash's tailgate as he pulled out. "Oh god. Dogs." He dashed from the barn to the yard and called Annabelle from the back door. "Hey, girl, you want to go out? It's going to snow again."

She ran out like she was on fire, and the puppies followed her, tumbling down the stairs in a pile. God, they were cute little dorks. He hung out on the back porch, watching them try to figure out the snow that was already on the ground, sniffing and pawing as they did their business. Annabelle was much more dignified, going out by the barn and coming back when she was done.

Then she came to him, snuggling up to get pets and love. She leaned against his leg, watching her puppies play and tumble and tackle each other. "They're going to be all wet, huh? Let's dry off your feet and then I'll haul them inside too." He grabbed a towel and went after her feet and her tummy, making sure she was clean and dry. "Shiloh should be home soon, right? I'll get the pups."

He'd finally managed to remember all of their names. Eighteen new students? No problem. Eight puppies? Forget it.

He ducked back outside, scooping them all up in his arms and bringing them inside to dry them off. Annabelle helped, nosing them and licking them. She was a great mom, he had to admit.

It would be better if Shiloh was home, though. He got the pups tucked into the laundry room and gave Annabelle a treat, then pulled out his phone to call.

The phone rang a few times, then he got voicemail. Dammit.

Well Shiloh was driving, right? Tate watched the snow out the front bay window. It was late afternoon now and starting to get dark, it was probably good that Shiloh hadn't answered. Safer.

Shiloh was getting better at driving in snow, but he wasn't a master, not by any means. He told himself he wasn't going to worry. The chores were all done so he'd make some popcorn, watch a movie or something and just be patient. Shiloh would probably be there before he got the movie going anyway.

Then they could snuggle and watch the snow fall together like a sappy romantic movie.

He squinted out the window one more time, then went to make popcorn. He called Shiloh again while it was popping and went to voicemail. This time he left one. "Hey, it's me. Just give me a call? It's snowing pretty hard and getting dark and... I know you're fine, but maybe call me to give your ETA? Love you."

When he got back out to the living room, Annabelle had her nose pressed to the bay window. "I know. He should be home soon." She didn't move. He plopped down on the couch and picked up the remote. "Come on, girl. It doesn't help to stare out the window. Plus, you're stressing me out. Sit."

She looked at him, came over and sat for petting, then went back to the window, watching.

"He'll be home soon. Maybe he stopped by Sky and Beckett's place." They weren't on the way home, but it also wouldn't be the first time Shiloh had run over there for something. Shiloh could have run in and left his phone in the truck.

He turned on the TV and put on the first movie he found.

Maybe he'd take a run down the road if Shiloh was gone much longer.

THE TRUCK HIT a patch of ice on the way home, and Shiloh was fucked.

Like nose in the ditch, resting against the steering wheel, not totally sure if he'd passed out or just knocked the wind out of himself. Dammit.

He wasn't sure how long of a walk he had, but he knew he had one. First, though, he needed to get himself out of the truck, call Tate, and get the groceries.

Right?

Right.

He had trees on the driver's side, so he killed the engine and climbed over to the passenger's side, praying that the door opened.

It took a little pushing, but that prayer was answered, and he climbed out, and was instantly covered in snow.

"Huh. I guess my next big ask is please let the phone have service." That was an ask too far, he guessed.

But the phone was working, so maybe if he got back on the road he'd find an open spot with enough to at least get a text through. He took a second to get his bearings because he wasn't sure which side of the road he'd slid off of. In all this snow, the road pretty much looked the same in both directions.

Okay. Okay. Up the hill had to be right, so he'd go for it.

Up it was. He climbed up the loose powder, sliding enough that his jeans were soaked by the time he was on his way up.

Where had this storm come from? Tate hadn't mentioned they were expecting a storm. It seemed to go from light to dim to dark in minutes, and he still had no cell service.

Okay. Fuck. Get on the road and…

Well, act like he had some sense, he guessed.

He'd stopped for a second to catch his breath when he spotted headlights coming up the hill in his direction. They kind of snuck up on him, looking far away at first and then a second later the truck was pulling up beside him. "Hey, man. You okay? Was that your truck back there? Get in. Get out of the snow."

"Jimmy?"

The kid blinked at him. "You're Mr. Dutton's guy! Were you heading home?"

"I had groceries." Shouldn't he grab them?

"They'll stay cold, trust me. Would you please get in the truck? You look like a snowman."

"I feel like one!" His legs and feet were frozen. "What are you doing out here?"

"I left work early trying to miss this, but..." Jimmy snorted. "If you can't feel your feet, kick your boots off. I've got a blanket..." Jimmy cranked the heat and reached into the back seat.

"Thanks. Can you—can you at least get me somewhere I can call home."

"Mr. Dutton is next. We'll stop there and call my dad." He got a nervous smile. "I'm cool, but I'd be cooler if he knew where I was."

"There's a guest room in the house, should you need it."

"Yeah, because that's not weird."

"We have puppies."

"Oh yeah. Mr. Dutton told us about them. He says they're cute."

He couldn't help his grin, because damn. He was the king of finding homes for beautiful pups. "We still have one that needs a home in a few weeks, you know."

"You do? I guess I could come in and see them."

"Great." *And stay, and have something warm for dinner, and go home in the morning when the roads are clearer.*

Jimmy handed him the blanket, then put the car in gear. "I need to get you home. Frostbite sucks."

They moved slowly but steadily toward the farm. Jimmy

didn't look intimidated by the snow, but he was concentrating on the road for sure.

Shiloh closed his eyes, trying not to shiver. He was colder now, somehow, than he had been out in the snow.

"How are your fingers? Keep wiggling them. Hey. Don't fall asleep either." Jimmy poked his arm. "We're almost there."

"I'm not sleeping. I'm just relaxing." Breathing.

Trying not to shake apart.

"Good, good okay. Oh, look. That's the house...look how pretty. Doesn't it look warm all lit up in the snow?" Jimmy approached the driveway and pulled in carefully. He'd barely put the truck in park before Tate appeared on the porch, squinting into the headlights.

"Mr. Dutton! Your...friend...was in an accident. I brought him home."

"Fiancé," he muttered. "I'm fine!"

"Shi? Jesus. Thank you, Jimmy! Shi, are you okay?" Tate waded through the snow to the truck. "You're soaked. Come in, quickly. Jimmy, come get warm."

Annabelle was going nuts, barking her little heart out from the living room.

"Fiancé? Oh! Oh cool. Cool." Jimmy held doors and otherwise looked pretty awkward.

"Yes, fiancé. Call your dad so he doesn't worry." Tate marched him right into the bedroom and through into the main bath, where Tate started the shower.

"Everything off, baby. Do you need help? God, you're so cold." Tate fussed over him, helping him undress.

"I'm okay. Just—not dressed for a blizzard walk." It would have been better if it hadn't come out as bliz-z-z-zard.

"No. Definitely not." His jeans were so frozen they left

snow and ice on the bathroom floor, but he managed to get out of them, and everything else. He could see Annabelle pacing in the bedroom as Tate put him in the shower, under the spray, and seemed to relax a little. "I was worried. I'm so glad you're home. Stay there and get warm, okay? I'm going to get out some dry clothes for you and clean this up."

"Okay. Sorry. What about Jimmy? Is he going to try and get home?"

"You hush and get warmed up. I'm glad you're home safe. I don't know about Jimmy; I haven't even talked to him yet, but I hope he stays put. What happened? Did you wreck your truck? Where did Jimmy come from?"

"I slid off the road into a ditch. I was trying to find signal on said road when he found me. I'm glad he stopped."

"Oh, Shi. How scary. I was trying to reach you; your phone is going to have a hundred voicemails and texts and... hold on." Tate disappeared, leaving him under the hot water with Annabelle watching him from the doorway. Tate came back after a moment and closed the bathroom door. "He's staying. He's watching TV." Tate stripped off and slid into the shower with him.

"Good deal. I hated thinking of him driving on alone." He reached for Tate almost immediately, drawing him into his arms.

"Cold... Jesus." Tate hugged him hard. "I tried not to worry, but that was hopeless. Stupid cell service. And it's so much worse in a storm."

"Yeah. I'm pretty sure the truck just needs a tow, you know? It was still running."

"We'll get a truck to come up tomorrow. Are you feeling warmer?" Tate's hands were sliding over his back, touching all his chilly skin.

"Yeah. I'm a little burny inside. That's normal, right? My body trying to warm up?"

"Sort of. You might be running a fever." Tate reached up and felt his ears. "Do they hurt at all? They look okay."

"No. No, they just feel hot. I wasn't out long enough to be hurt. Just chilled. I left the groceries in the truck."

"Well, they won't go bad." Tate chuckled, then leaned up and kissed him. "Hey. Are you hungry?"

He wasn't, but he knew that saying so would worry Tate. "I am."

"Okay. We need to feed Jimmy anyway." Tate was talking, but not moving, he still had a tight hold of Shiloh's waist.

He rested down on Tate's shoulder, letting himself relax. "That was a little unnerving."

"You're home now." Tate took a deep breath, like that small admission was something he'd needed. "That storm came up fast and out of nowhere. It was supposed to be much later tonight."

"Yeah. I checked the weather before I left, even." He turned his face, and kissed Tate, long and slow and sweet, just saying hi and I'm home and yay.

"Mm. I think you're finally warming up," Tate said, lips still brushing against his.

"Yes. I'm feeling like I can stop shivering." And like he was home.

"I want to keep you right here and make sure you're plenty toasty, but we have a young house guest." Tate chuckled. "So, I'm going to get you into some warm sweats and socks and a hoodie and stick you in front of the fire."

"Yeah, it's totally a bad teacher moment to get it on like that." It would be a funny damn story to tell Sky though.

"Maybe after he's gone to bed..." Tate tucked a hand around his perfectly warm balls.

His toes curled, and he rocked into the touch. "I promise to be very, very quiet."

"Good boy." Tate grinned and let him go. "Okay. Dinner for the teenager, maybe some cocoa, maybe a movie." He got another kiss before Tate climbed out of the shower. "I love you, you know."

"I hope so. I intend to marry you and raise a family."

"Good thing you didn't freeze your nuts off, then." Tate handed him a big, fluffy towel.

"You'd love me nutless." Did he really just say that?

"I would. But it's hard to have kids without them." Tate winked at him.

"You want it to be me?" He'd never once thought that. He'd assumed—Tate was a teacher, was so clever and handsome...

"Mhm. I do. I want a handful of little Shilohs running around." Tate pulled him out of the shower. "Dry off, you need to get dressed."

"Yes, boss." He laughed and toweled off, hurrying to wrap up so he didn't freeze. "Thank you, babe."

Tate narrowed his eyes, but his grin was playful. "That's right, you should be grateful considering how much you worried me. And I thought Annabelle was going to have a stroke."

"Poor little pup. She loves me."

"She does." Tate was handing him clothing—socks, undies, sweats, T-shirt—and Annabelle was sniffing him all over.

"Hey, sweet baby. I would never leave you. Ever."

She licked his hand and backed off as Tate handed him a sweatshirt.

"Okay. Warmer? You want some coffee? You sure you're hungry? We need to feed Jimmy something anyway."

"I would love a cup of coffee. Please." He stole another kiss.

Jimmy hopped up off the couch as they came into the room. "Hey. You look warmer. My parents say thank you."

"Hey, you got Shiloh home to me, thank *you*."

"Of course. That's scary, right? Being in a wreck at night..." Jimmy grinned at him, gave him a wink.

"I bet it is." Tate snorted. "Come on, let's make you something to eat. Shiloh cooks, so there's tons of leftovers. Or we can make some pasta. Or scramble some eggs..."

"There's bacon too. I'll make carbonara." Comforting, warm, and filling.

"Ooh. Fancy." Jimmy was impressed.

"I'm supposed to be pampering you, snowman."

"You can make me coffee."

Tate gave Jimmy an apologetic look. "You really can't trust me to make much else. Shiloh spoils me."

Jimmy looked sympathetic. "My dad doesn't cook at all. Mom says he can burn water."

"That's actually fairly impressive, when you think about it," he teased. "I'd have to work at that one."

"I'm pretty good. I can help. Just tell me what to do." Jimmy rolled up his sleeves.

"Chop up bacon? That would be perfect." Shiloh found Jimmy a cutting board and a knife.

Jimmy got to work, chopping like someone had taken some time to teach him, and Tate put on some music, then filled the coffee pot with water.

Shiloh was warm, clean, dry, and home. Tomorrow he'd figure out what to do with his truck and the groceries, but first he'd cook supper and then see if Tate was still interested in a nice, quiet orgasm with the door locked.

It would be worth getting left out in the cold.

24

Tate lay on his back, eyes wide open, staring at the ceiling. His mind was racing—what about the truck? What if Shiloh was actually hurt and just didn't feel it yet?

What if Jimmy hadn't come along?

He sighed. He'd been just about ready to get in his own ride to go find Shiloh himself when Jimmy's truck appeared. Then it would have been both of them out in the snow.

He didn't want to think about it.

But he was. He couldn't get his stupid brain to stop thinking about what might have happened.

Shiloh sighed and turned over, one hand landing on his stomach, heavy and warm.

He curled in, resting his head on Shi's bent arm. He didn't need to think about what could have happened, because it hadn't. And Shi was right here, so solid, and smelling so good. "I love you," he whispered and kissed Shi's scratchy jaw.

His words made Shiloh smile, the soft hum pure sex. "Mmm... Baby. You're so warm."

"Yeah. You too." He didn't think twice this time, letting his fingers slide over Shi's abs, playing across the ridges.

The husky chuckle slid down his spine and settled down south. Damn, that was fine. "Mmm. Ticklish?"

"More sensitive. I like it." Shiloh caught his lips, kissing him softly. "A lot."

"Yeah?" He kept touching, more deliberate about it this time. Jimmy was sound asleep by now, right? "I'm feeling a little sensitive too."

"Are you? Are you experiencing a little...stiffness." Shiloh chuckled, the sound tickled and so sweet.

"A little. You want to check it out for me? I think this condition might be going around." He coaxed another one of those kisses out of Shiloh, fingers searching for the sensitive spot on Shi's hip.

"Oh no..." Shiloh chuckled, even as he bucked into Tate's fingers. "You'll distract me."

"Distracting you sounds like a great idea." He needed the distraction himself. He blew a raspberry against Shiloh's neck and stroked his fingers over that spot again.

That drew out a volley of chuckles, along with a gasp. "Do you th-think so?"

"This is no laughing matter, my friend." He slid his hand lower, into Shi's soft curls and lower, to fondle that heavy sac.

"Oh, we're not just friends. We're way more." Shiloh stared at him, lips parted and hungry.

"Way more, baby." He kissed those lips and caught Shi's cock in his palm, then slowly curled his fingers around the shaft.

Shiloh grunted for him, the sound wild when it pushed against his lips.

"Shh... This is quiet time, babe."

That was easy for him to say; he just needed to remember that himself when the time came. No scandalizing his student.

He squeezed Shiloh's prick, then let it go so he could tease, fingers gliding lightly up the shaft, palm ghosting over the head, his thigh tucking up under Shiloh's balls.

"Uhn." That sound was a mere whisper. "Babe."

"Is that good?" he whispered back. "I've just been lying here wanting you." That wasn't entirely true, he'd been lying there trying not to worry about Shiloh mostly, but it sounded hotter than the truth.

"You should have woken me. I always want you. Always."

He felt the same way. He gripped that thick cock again and rocked a little, finding it hard to keep still. "Good to know."

"Mmhmm...but we're here now." Shiloh's muscles rippled, and a groan tore from him.

"You're definitely awake." He rolled them and straddled Shiloh, smiling down at his fiancé. "Remember, quiet now."

"Qu-quiet. I remember." Shiloh sucked in a deep breath, filling his lungs.

He loved teasing his lover, turning him on. He couldn't believe he could really drive this gorgeous man a little crazy. He never thought of himself that way and Shiloh could be so stoic.

"Good boy."

Ha. Listen to him.

He bent to one tight, pink nub and drew his tongue across it.

"I'll show you good boy." Shiloh chuckled and grabbed his cock, jacking him with a firm hand.

"Fuck," Tate swore as his prick filled fast and sparkles

spun before his eyes like pinwheels. "Fuck, that's got to be cheating."

"Uh-huh. Totally." Shiloh laughed for him, the sound husky and low, pure sex.

"I can cheat too, you know." He returned the favor, swooping his fingers up Shiloh's length and burying his thumb in that slippery slit in the swollen head.

Shiloh responded with an arch and a muffled cry that vibrated against his skin.

"Jesus, Shi. That was the hottest thing ever," he whispered and leaned forward for a kiss.

"Your fault." Shiloh groaned deep in his chest, then smiled against his shoulder. "Do it again."

He grinned too, enjoying the playful side of Shiloh. "Fuck yeah. Okay, baby." He repeated the gesture, swiping root to tip and pushing that little slit wide open. That earned him another full-body shudder, a roll of the hips.

"Fuck me, that's intense." Shiloh's fist tightened on his cock, moving a little faster.

He nodded, taking in a shaky breath. "Do you...one better." He snatched the lube off the nightstand and waggled it at Shiloh before popping open the lid.

"Ooh..." Shiloh bit his bottom lip. "Right. Quiet. Shh."

He slicked Shi's prick with a practiced hand. He wasn't sure exactly when they'd stopped using rubbers, but they had given them up naturally like they'd done everything else. "Shh or I won't ride you like the fuzzy pony you are."

"That would be a shame, sweetheart. I swear to god." Shi's face went lax as he stroked and petted. Tate loved that expression, the way Shiloh's lips parted on a moan.

"So hot, baby." He rose up and got into position, then slowly sank down, eyes crossing with the glorious stretch and burn. Fuck, it was his favorite part. He bit his lips together to keep the sound in and took Shiloh in even farther. He craved this, and Shiloh went deep, filling him up and making him gasp.

"Jesus..." There was no way he was going to be able to keep quiet. No fucking way. Except he had to. "Shi..."

"Kiss me." Shiloh tugged him down and slammed their mouths together, shutting him up and driving into him in the same motions.

He groaned into the kiss. Fuck, yeah, this was going to work. They'd just breathe each other's air. He leaned into the kiss and rocked down to meet those hungry thrusts.

He grabbed hold of Shiloh's shoulders, fingertips digging in as Shiloh grabbed his hips and thrust up with short, sharp strokes.

He felt his climax brewing suddenly, out of nowhere and he breathed in Shiloh's scent, rubbed his cheek against that scratchy face and leaned back just enough to look into those bottomless dark eyes. "Love you."

"Love you, baby. Come for me." Shiloh wrapped one hand around his cock and pumped twice, nice and firm.

He nodded and took another crazy kiss, filling Shi's lungs with his shout as he came.

Shi stroked him through his aftershocks, then started pushing hard, fucking him in short, hard thrusts that made his eyes cross as Shiloh fought for his own completion.

Tate saw his lover's expression go lax, and then he felt heat pulsing into him, filling him. He stayed there for a bit, breathing and feeling everything. He couldn't stop his grin —that had been ridiculous and hot at the same time. "Fuck," he whispered finally, like that one word said it all.

"Uh-huh." Shiloh totally had babyhead against the pillows. "Also wow."

He chuckled and shifted, stretching out long beside that tough, strong body. "You're a sexy fucker."

"You make my eyes cross." Shi turned with a soft, happy sigh, snuggling in.

"I do like you a bit louder..." He tickled Shi's armpit.

Shiloh snorted, grabbing him and tickling his ribs. "Be good, now."

"Don't. Don't...do not. Go to sleep. Stop!" He was still whispering but just barely. He slapped at Shiloh's hand, and the sound was loud and sharp. "Oops."

"You're going to have to explain, you know..."

"Nightmare. A nightmare named Shiloh." He sighed, limbs getting heavy.

"Oh, good deal. Great idea." Shiloh sighed softly, humming under his breath, and the sigh became snores.

"Best nightmare ever." More like a dream he didn't ever want to wake up from. He kissed Shiloh's chest and closed his eyes.

25

"Let me straighten your tie, man." Sky reached up and fixed the ends of his bolo tie while Charlie galloped around him in her best barrel racer costume.

She was so fine, in her jeans and sparkly hat and belt, and she'd be the best grooms-cowgirl of all time, standing with her daddy, who was his best man.

Sierra was the flower girl, Noah was their ring bearer, and Annabelle was the best dog ever.

The puppies were still sort of in asshole mode, so they were in the dog run.

"Are you excited?"

Shiloh nodded, because he was. The weather was beautiful. The greenhouse and the garden were blooming, and they were—stupidly happy. "It's sure different from my first one, huh?"

"It was a different world. Matty was a different guy. Sure it's different."

Matty was a different guy. That was the understatement of the century. There was almost nothing about Tate that was like Matty.

"This is good, Shiloh, you know that? He's good for you. He's a partner. And Beckett likes him, so there's that."

"I like him too. I want to spend the rest of my life with him." And that was enough. It was more than enough.

"Good because Tate is stressing, man." Nash poked his head into the bedroom. "He's out there looking handsome and nervous, but I think he's worried that you're going to change your mind. Think I should get him a shot of something?"

"Tell him I'm meeting him outside. We can walk down the aisle together, after the kids go. Fair?"

"I'll tell him." Nash gave him a huge grin. "Congrats man. See you out there."

"It's all good." And he believed that. It was going to be theirs—their day, their wedding, their new life.

"I don't know what he's worried about, you're hooked by the balls." Sky chuckled and pinned a flower to his lapel.

"It's his first time." And, please God, it would be their last. "We'll forgive some nerves."

Sky smoothed out his lapels. "Oh, you're all wisdom and experience, huh?"

"In an hour I'll have been married twice as many times as you..."

"Ha. I guess that does make you an expert." Sky laughed and patted his shoulder. "Are you ready?"

"As ready as I'll ever be." He took a deep breath and opened the door.

"Let's go." Sky led the way and held the door open for him. They had some chairs but mostly their few guests were standing in the sunshine in their backyard. The simple, square wedding arch he'd built looked great against the barn in the background and someone, probably Beckett, had covered it in flowers.

Music was playing, and Sky and Nash started assembling the kids.

Tate made his way over, looking about as nervous as Nash had said, but smiling anyway. His hair was a perfectly deliberate mess and his gray suit fit him just right. "Hey, you. We're going to do this, huh?"

He leaned down, stealing a soft, warm kiss. "We are. Are you ready, honey, because I sure am."

"Now that you're here, looking that good? I am so ready."

Sky sent Charlie down the aisle.

"I can't wait to see if Sierra remembers how to throw the flower petals," he whispered. "Or if Noah eats the rings."

"Or if Annabelle lets them get all the way down the aisle without trying to herd them." Tate chuckled and took his arm. "I'm here for it. All of it—from honeymoon to babies and beyond."

It would be an adventure. The first of the rest of their lives. They were planting the seeds, and all their love needed was sunshine and them working together to keep it on track.

"I'm all in."

THE WRECKED UNIVERSE

Read the Wrecked Novels

Wrecked

Flying Blind

Special Delivery

Seeds and Sunshine

Interested in learning more about BA's cowboys and Jodi's gentlemen? Want free fiction and news? Join our newsletters!

What's Up with Jodi
https://readerlinks.com/l/2317334

Spurs and Shifters
https://lp.constantcontact.com/su/A9CRUzp/baandjulia

Howdy, Y'all!

We want to thank you for giving Seeds and Sunshine a try. We hope you enjoyed the story.

If you can spare a few minutes to post a review at the retail website where you made your purchase, we'd very much appreciate it!

Don't forget to "like" our Facebook pages and groups to keep up with all the news--new releases, sales announcements, giveaways, sneak peeks-- and of course the rodeo pictures, coffee memes and just general fun. We'd love to have all y'all!

Yeehaw and thanks for reading!

BA & Jodi

ABOUT JODI

JODI takes herself way too seriously and has been known to randomly break out in song. Her men are imperfect but genuine, stubborn but likable, often kinky, and frequently their own worst enemies. They are characters you can't help but fall in love with while they stumble along the path to their happily ever after. For those looking to get on her good side, Jodi's addictions include nonfat lattes, Malbec and tequila any way you pour it.

Website: jodipayne.net
Newsletter: https://readerlinks.com/l/2317334
All Jodi's Social Links: linktr.ee/jodipayne

ABOUT BA

Western to the bone and an unrepentant Daddy's Girl, BA Tortuga spends her days with her hounds and her beloved wife, having mother-daughter dates, and eating Mexican food. When she's not doing that, she's writing. She spends her days off watching rodeo, knitting, and surfing Pinterest in the name of research. Following their own personal joys, BA and Julia heard the call of the high desert and they now live in the New Mexico mountains. BA's personal saviors include her wife, her best friends, and coffee. Lots of coffee. Really good coffee.

Having written everything from fist-fighting cowboys to rural single dads to werewolves, BA does her damnedest to tell the stories of her heart, which is committed to giving everyone their happily ever after. With books ranging from heart-warming stories of found families, to rodeo cowboys that are fighting to make a mark, to fiery passionate love affairs, BA refuses to be pigeon-holed by anyone but the voices in her head.

BA loves to talk to her readers and can be found at http://batortuga.com/ and her newsletter signup link is http://bit.ly/BAJulianews